PREGNANT BY THE ALIEN HEALER

WARRIORS OF THE LATHAR

MINA CARTER

Copyright © 2017 by Mina Carter

All rights reserved.

No part of this book may be reproduced in any form or by any electronic or mechanical means, including information storage and retrieval systems, without written permission from the author, except for the use of brief quotations in a book review.

CONTENTS

Chapter 1	1
Chapter 2	15
Chapter 3	31
Chapter 4	49
Chapter 5	67
Chapter 6	79
Chapter 7	95
Chapter 8	109
Chapter 9	125
Chapter 10	139
Chapter 11	153
Chapter 12	171
Chapter 13	185
Chapter 14	197
Chapter 15	213
Chapter 16	229
Chapter 17	245
Chapter 18	259
Read an excerpt from ALIEN COMMANDER'S MATE...	271
About the Author	281

1

"So, they're *both* princes?"

Jessica Kallson, Jess to her friends, sipped her drink and watched the small group of men on the other side of the room.

Unlike Jess and the two women standing next to her, they weren't human. Standing well over six feet apiece, with more muscles than she'd ever seen on a man, they were Lathar, the warrior race who had attacked and captured the frontier defense base she'd been stationed on.

Since then, relations had warmed somewhat. Not quite captives anymore, Jess and the other women who'd been brought to the Imperial Court on Lathar Prime were now treated as honored guests of the emperor.

The emperor with the *very* nice ass in his tight warrior's leathers she was ogling as he greeted the two men in front of him—both his nephews. But her attention didn't remain on Daaynal, the emperor, for long. Instead it was hijacked by one of the other men.

Laarn K'Vass was identical to his brother, the husband of Jess' best friend Cat, but where Tarrick's hair was cut short, Laarn's was long. Where Tarrick wore the red sash of a war commander, Laarn's was the teal that denoted he was a healer. There were other differences as well. His eyes were green, not gold like Tarrick's, and the body under the jacket Laarn wore buttoned to his neck was badly scarred. The scars were from his profession. She'd only seen them once, brutal marks that decorated his lean, hard body like artwork.

"Hmmm... say what?" She blinked as Cat, standing next to her, clicked her fingers in front of Jess' face.

"If you can tear your eyes away from my brother-in-law for a moment," Cat chuckled, amusement on her face. "I said that yes, they're both technically princes. Their mother was Daaynal's *litaan,* his twin."

"Huh," Jess started a little in surprise. "I didn't realize they had male-female twin sets."

"Yeah. At least, they used to." Cat sighed. "But with girl babies dying in the womb... there haven't been any born for a long time."

Jess nodded, silent at the reminder that for all their military might, the Lathar were facing doomsday as a species. She swirled the drink in her glass and continued watching the three men. Well, she continued watching Laarn as he stepped aside from his brother and uncle, leaving them to talk. She'd noticed that about him.

Although he was as big-built and muscular as his brother, he often stepped back out of the way when Tarrick was talking, as though not wanting to take the attention. He wasn't shy, though. She'd seen him training and interacting with the other warriors, and he had an easy aura of command they all obeyed. He was quieter, but no less alpha for it. It was more a quiet power, as he watched all around him with a critical eye, and it sent shivers down her spine.

"He's going to see you looking soon, you know?" Cat commented, her eyes alight with amusement as she looked over the rim of her glass.

Like Jess' it was filled with a Champagne-type

drink, but lilac in color. And, unlike Champagne, she'd found it didn't give her a hellish hangover in the morning. That wasn't to say it wasn't strong. Already she felt a little merry, so she always made sure only to drink one or two glasses. While they were "honored guests" of the court, there were more than enough dangers to watch out for...

Unbidden, her gaze slid to the other side of the room where a large group of warriors had congregated. Most of them were drinking and laughing amongst themselves, and... yes, there was a fight going on in the far corner. Nothing serious by the looks of it, just a friendly bout between two warriors. In the middle, though, one warrior stood steadfast and silent, his light gaze fixed on her. Saal.

Quickly Jess looked away, not making eye contact. Saal had been pursuing her since they'd arrived on Lathar Prime, the fact that he'd happily claim her for his own clear. But, handsome as the guy was, Jess' attentions lay elsewhere. With a tall, handsome healer...

Her gaze returned to Laarn, who also had a drink in his large hand. But he wasn't drinking it. Instead, all his attention was on the pad in his hand. A sheet of flexible plastic, it was the Lathar equivalent of a computer and cell phone all rolled into one, but it could be folded up and slipped into a pocket.

"I doubt he'll even notice, or care much." She buried her nose into her glass and took another drink, hating the hurt little sound in her voice.

Laarn was a healer and dedicated to his work. He probably hadn't noticed her, or the fact she was a woman. His entire interest in her was solely based on the fact she was Terran.

She'd tried to chat with him when she'd been in the medbay, offering to spend countless hours in the high-tech hologram bed thing in there as he scanned her DNA over and over, but he'd only ever talked about medical issues. What was her medical history, had she had any diseases in her lifetime, had anyone in her family had anything unusual?

He'd been fascinated when she'd told him about cancer, even though it had all but been eradicated, and about childhood diseases. As soon as she tried to get something personal out of him though, he clammed up, declared they were done for the day and left medical.

She'd soon learned not to ask him anything personal, in the hope of spending more time with him. Perhaps if he saw her often enough, he might start seeing her as a woman.

So far, though, no such luck.

"Hmmm... yeah, he's very focused on his work," Cat admitted, a frown between her brows. The frown was noticed as they were joined by a third woman, her fingers laced through that of a tall, heavily built warrior. Jane Allen had been the Marine commander on the base but was now happily married to one of their former captors, Karryl.

"Who is? What did I miss?" Jane asked, her gaze following the direction they were both suddenly not looking in. She sighed. "Laarn? Is he *still* being obtuse?"

"Obtuse? What is this word?" Karryl looked around the small group, his expression curious as, obviously not satisfied with just holding Jane's hand, he wrapped his arm around her waist and pulled her into his side.

"It means he's being dense," Jane explained, her hand on the broad chest of her man. Jess all but sighed at the loved-up look the two exchanged. She wanted that, the all-consuming love and passion she saw between Cat and Tarrick and now Jane and Karryl. "It means he's not seeing what's standing right there in front of him. In this case, Jess."

Karryl blinked, the surprise evident. "But she

isn't standing in front of him. She's standing right here."

"No, that's not what I me—" Jane paused as she clocked the tiny curve at the corner of his lips. "Asshole. You know what I mean."

He grinned. "I do. But why do you think he doesn't see her? Laarn's a healer, but he's as male as the rest of us. I think you'll find he's probably *very* aware of Jess."

"He is?" Cat and Jess asked at the same time. Then Cat gestured toward where the big healer stood, his attention still riveted on the pad in his hand. "How does that equate to being aware of Jess?"

Karryl's expression went blank for the moment in a neutral expression Jess had noticed a lot of the warriors used, usually when they didn't want to talk. He shrugged. "A man is a man, whatever else he does."

LAARN HATED SOCIAL FUNCTIONS. They were pointless. A waste of time that could be better spent elsewhere, doing something productive or in the training arena.

He sighed as he looked up at the sounds of a

fight. Seemed like some warriors had decided to bring the training arena here. A small group hovered around a pair who were going at it hammer and tongs. The betting had already started. By the looks of the combatants though, and the quick glances they kept shooting across the other side of the room, they were less interested in the winner's cut and more interested in catching the eye of one of the human women.

Bloody show offs, Laarn snorted to himself, but he couldn't resist a quick look that way himself. There were nearly twenty of them at court now, and all delightfully feminine in a way the Lathar, without women of their own, hadn't seen in decades. The fact that they were the descendants of a Lathar colony team only added to their allure.

Even he could see the appeal. They were tiny but intelligent, and some were as fierce as any warrior. Not that all males found that kind of fierceness attractive. Some did. His gaze fell on the tall figure of his lifelong friend, Karryl.

From the same clan, they shared blood on their father's side and had grown up together. The big warrior had his arm wrapped around the slender waist of his new mate, the human warrioress, Jane Allan. Laarn had seen her in battle, and she was as ruthless as any Lathar. He'd heard tale that she'd shot the warrior who'd poisoned Karryl and tried to claim her point blank between the eyes, not a shred of mercy in her body. Karryl beamed with pride as he looked down at his mate, obviously head over heels in love, with his wrists bare to show off his mating marks.

But, for all that he'd been brought up a warrior before going down the path of healer, Laarn didn't want such a warrior woman for himself. His gaze slid to the side a little, to a slender woman standing between Karryl's mate and his brother's mate, Cat.

Jessica Kallson.

For a moment, he was frozen in place, watching in fascination as she turned to place her empty glass on the tray of an *oonat,* a waitress. The light conspired and highlighted the slender curve of her neck and jaw, his gaze riveting to the luscious line of her lips as she smiled at something Karryl had said.

Jealousy ripped through him in an instant, his fists clenched at his side as he glared across the room. The only man she should be looking at, smiling at, was *him.*

"She's a pretty little thing. Isn't she?"

Laarn turned slightly to find Daaynal standing next to him. Slightly taller and heavier than Laarn himself, he had the same green eyes Laarn saw in the mirror each morning.

"She appears to be attractive for her species, yes."

He returned his attention to Jess, immediately tapping down his reaction to the little human female. Daaynal might appear to most to be a big, dumb warrior, but Laarn knew better. His uncle was as ruthless as the day was long and far cannier than he appeared. He'd survived countless assassination attempts since he'd been on the Imperial throne, and many before that, when he'd been a crown prince. There were even rumors that he'd killed his first assassin before he was ten cycles old, saving both himself and his sister, Laarn's mother, in the process.

"Attractive for her species?" Daaynal snorted, burying his nose in his tankard and taking a deep swallow. "Have you heard yourself? *Attractive?* She's beautiful. They all are..." He lifted his head to look across the room at the group of women, warm appreciation in his eyes.

When he looked back, his gaze was sharp. He looked over Laarn's shoulder for a moment, pointedly, and then back again.

"Careful that the prize you want isn't stolen out from under your nose while you're not looking, sister-son," he advised in a low voice. "Now, tell me of your research."

Laarn groaned inwardly. He'd hoped Daaynal wouldn't ask, but he kept his expression neutral.

"So far the genetic material confirms that the Terrans are descendants of the lost exploratory mission. There is some deviation, but after so long that's to be expected."

"They're still close enough genetically to us though?" Daaynal asked.

Laarn nodded. "Yes, they are. Procreation between human and Lathar is more than possible, expected even. In fact," he mused, looking across the room to where the two human-Lathar couples were standing, "since the bonded males can't keep their hands off their mates, I'm surprised we haven't seen a pregnancy yet."

He managed to keep the frustration out of his voice. Just. As the premier healer in the Latharian empire, he was leading the research project into the condition that caused all female young to die in the womb. Because without women of their own, they were doomed as a race. Even with the influx of human women, there was always the possibility that the same thing could happen to any human-Lathar children. If it did, gaining human mates for their warriors was at best simply a stay of execution. In less than a generation, they would be facing the same problem.

And that wasn't the worst of it. He'd been tracking the problem with their DNA for years, and it was speeding up. If his suspicions were correct, before too long it wouldn't just be the female fetuses that were affected. It would be any viable fetus. And shortly after, the ability of any warrior to get his woman pregnant would be eradicated.

"I just don't get it," he added. "It's not progressing like any disease I've ever seen before. If I had to guess from the raw data, I'd say we were looking at more of a bio-genetic agent at work, but on a massive scale with no clue as to the method of infection."

He sighed, running his hand through his hair in a rare display of agitation. He was a good healer, a damn good one. Probably the best in the empire and, some said, better than even his grandfather, the last, near-legendary lord healer. Some said, but not all. More said he wasn't as good as his grandfather, that the K'Vass line was muddied by the fact the lord healer had married a commoner. Never where any K'Vass warrior could hear, of course—no Lathar was *that* suicidal—but he knew what they said.

He couldn't heal them.

"You'll find something," Daaynal said, belief in his voice. "Although, wouldn't it be easier if you had a mate of your own... for close observational purposes, of course. You'd be able to monitor any possible pregnancy in real-time, wouldn't you?"

Oh, his uncle was good. Laarn almost found himself nodding in agreement before he stopped dead. Even the flicker of an eyelid might be taken by Daaynal to mean he agreed, and thus seal his... and Jess'... fate. He allowed his gaze to flick over to her. She was so tiny and delicate compared to him. When he was around her, he ached to claim her. But he couldn't. And he couldn't allow Daaynal to remove her choices either and make her mate him.

He'd seen the looks on the human women's faces when he'd removed his jacket during the journey to court. The shock and then the careful looks away. Or if any of them had to look at him, they ensured they looked him directly in the eye, no quick glances down to his body.

For the first time in his life, he'd been concerned about how others viewed him. How *Jess* viewed him. Did she see the strength it had taken to endure the marks he carried? Or did she see him as a scarred monster?

His jaw tightened. From the way the humans

acted around him, it had to be the latter. He was under no illusions. He wasn't pretty to look at. And, if their species treasured physical appearance so much, why would she want him when there were better looking warriors around?

"Think about it," Daaynal ordered, clapping him on the back and then moving away to circulate.

Laarn stood where he was a few moments longer and then turned with a sigh. He should make an effort and talk to a few people. Then, at the first opportunity, he would make his escape and return to the lab.

He had work to do if he was going to save them all.

2

Laarn had disappeared on her yet again.

Jess sighed in frustration as she slipped from the ballroom unnoticed and made her way toward where she was sure he would be.

His lab. She sighed. Seriously, the guy took workaholic to the next level and then some. Attached to the med-bay, he seemed to spend most of his time in there. So much so, she was sure he either had a pallet set up in his office, or he simply didn't sleep.

If she had to guess, she'd say the latter. Sometimes he looked bone-weary tired. Hot as hell, but tired down to his soul despite the determined aura that surrounded him like a cape.

Biting her lip, she turned the corridor. She just

wished he'd turn some of that determination on her, the way Tarrick had with Cat, or Karryl with Jane. With the latter couple, Jane had wanted nothing to do with Karryl, but the big alien warrior had persevered, stuck at it like a terrier with a bone and not given up on getting the woman he wanted.

Now they were happily married... or mated... Whatever you wanted to call it, they were it. All she knew was that Jane had a ring on her finger and Karryl had tattoo-like marks around his wrists all the other warriors looked at with envy. It was a love story from beyond the stars... and her silly romantic heart couldn't help sighing and wanting that herself.

Her slippered footsteps were near silent in the high vaulted corridors. Like the Lathar ships, the Imperial Palace was built on a much bigger scale than anything she was used to, but then, so were they. She was getting used to it though. She'd always been a little bit claustrophobic in space, sometimes feeling the metal walls and bulkheads were pressing in on her, but not on a Lathar ship. Not with all the wide open spaces and high corridors.

Yeah, she could get used to living in a place like this, leaving the dirt and dust of the crowded human colonies behind...

As she looked up a tall, leather-clad figure

stepped into the corridor, just before she reached the double doors to the medbay, and blocked her path.

Saal. *Again.*

She came to a stop, the long sweep of her skirts disguising the fact she'd almost skidded to avoid running into him. The Lathar were touchy-feely if they could get away with it, but mostly only if contact was initiated first. Bumping into, brushing up against, stepping close to... all counted as initiation, and she really didn't want to go there with Saal. Like *really* didn't want to go there. The keen look in his eyes and the determination said that would only end one way—with him trying to formally claim her in front of the court.

According to the weird rules the Lathar worked by, she could only refuse a claim three times before it got ugly. Originally, when they'd first been taken, the human women had been warned they'd end up in one of the pleasure houses—prostitutes used over and again by any warrior that walked through the door. Now they were under Daaynal's protection, she doubted it would come to that, but she'd probably be sent home. Away from the alien culture she was starting to love... away from Laarn.

No way. No how.

"Good evening." She inclined her head, trying to

imitate the cool elegance she'd noticed Cat use around the Lathar warriors. Her voice came out breathy and cutesy.

Dammit, where was her inner bitch when she needed her? There was no way she could do what Cat did, her graceful manner a far cry from Jess' bumbling ineptitude. They'd been friends for years, but at times she was envious of her beautiful, slender friend for her poise and grace. She loved Cat to bits, but she was so perfect... and Laarn was Tarrick's twin, presumably with a similar upbringing and likely the same tastes. Probably why Laarn didn't see Jess as a woman.

"Good evening? It would be a good evening if you would allow me to spend time with you." Saal smiled as he stepped closer. Jess resisted the temptation to step back. It would be an admission of fear and she knew better than to show fear to a predator. Even one that walked on two legs like a Lathar warrior... *especially* one that walked on two legs like a Lathar warrior.

His gaze flickered over her hair, her face, and downward, over her figure encased in the floating robe-like dress of a Lathar woman. Pleasure flashed over his features. "You are the most beautiful female I have ever seen."

Probably one of the only females he'd seen in recent years, the snarky voice in the back of her head added.

She ignored it, inclining her head in thanks for his compliment. Warlike they might be, but Latharian society did have rules and etiquette, and the human women had discovered the best way to deal with them at times was with politeness and formality.

Saal stepped closer, almost into her personal space, and she froze as he leaned in. "I want you, little human female, and I intend to have you," he murmured in a deep voice, his lips not far from her ear. "You can run as much as you like, but you will be mine."

The shiver rolled down her spine and she'd taken a step back before she could stop it. The feral smile that curved his lips said he'd seen the small movement. Fuck.

"Not this evening, she won't," a cold voice sounded from behind him.

Saal turned quickly to reveal Laarn standing in the doorway of the medbay, his arms folded over a broad chest. The look on his face was hard as he looked at Saal, but it softened somewhat as his gaze flicked to Jessica.

"Miss Kallson, thank you for coming so promptly. The test we were talking about is now ready." He stepped slightly to the side, sweeping an arm toward the open door behind him. "If you would step this way?"

She could have kissed him out of sheer relief, sweeping past the hulking form of Saal where he almost filled the corridor and into the safety of the medbay behind Laarn. She turned just in time to see the look of fury that crossed the other warrior's face as he squared up to Laarn. The temperature in the corridor dropped a couple of degrees. Although the healer hadn't moved, the set of his body and the sudden tension in his frame said he was more than happy to meet violence with violence should Saal offer it.

Holding her breath, she waited as the two men locked gazes, a tremor running down her spine. She'd seen challenge fights erupt between warriors over the slightest little thing, and they were always brutal. But fights over women seemed to be something else.

She'd only seen one, when they'd first arrived on Lathar Prime and a warrior had taken a liking to Jane. The fight between him and Karryl had been furious and ruthless, and it had nearly claimed

Karryl's life when the other guy cheated. Karryl only survived because one of the women, not giving two hoots about the warriors' honor code, pulled a gun on the challenger and threatened to blow his brains out.

But the three of them were the only ones here, and she didn't have a gun. Saal didn't back down, taking a half step toward the big healer. The tension between them was electric. She wouldn't have been surprised to see sparks flying between them as Laarn dropped his hands to his sides.

"You want to do this?" the healer growled, his voice far lower and more dangerous than Jess had ever heard it before. The rough edge and tones shivered over her skin, the sound turning her on. Hell, what was wrong with her? A guy's voice alone shouldn't turn her on this much.

Laarn lifted a hand, and the sound of tearing fabric filled the corridor as he ripped open his jacket, shrugging it off to dump it on the floor at his feet. Jess caught her gasp as his body was revealed, all hard, ripped muscle and scars over every inch of skin. The power there turned her on, even as what he'd been through made her heart ache. The scars were from his healer's trials, where he'd suffered through every disease, ailment and surgery he would treat as a healer. In the Lathar tradition, the more pain a healer could take, the higher their level of training.

Laarn was a lord healer... the highest level of doctor they had. *The* highest-ranking healer in the empire.

Saal's expression shifted as he saw the scars, his eyes widening imperceptibly. His skin paled a little as he inclined his head.

"My apologies, Lord Healer. I meant no offense. I merely wish to protect Lady Jessica."

Laarn clenched his fists, white showing over his knuckles. "That duty is not yours to assume. Lady Jessica and the other Terran women are under the protection of the emperor, and by extension, his family. *Me.* Leave. Now. Before you overstep your bounds, warrior." Laarn practically spat the words.

Saal backed up before he started to step forward, ducking his head. "Of course, Lord Healer. My apologies," he muttered, and turning, disappeared down the corridor.

Jess sagged a little, her hip against the nearest diagnostic bed as relief washed through her hard and fast that it hadn't come to a fight.

"Oh my goodness, thank you." Her voice was soft, heartfelt, as the double doors to the medbay shut at a wave of Laarn's hand. She'd seen the gesture many times before, but not the one that followed it. The door turned red, indicating he'd locked it.

"You shouldn't thank me," Laarn's voice was a growl as he turned and she sucked in a hard breath at the look on his face. "All you've managed to do is shut yourself in with a worse danger. *Me.*"

ANGER ROLLED THROUGH HIM, hard and fast, at the danger Jess had put herself in. Why she'd left the ballroom without an escort he had no idea, but it just proved how *draanthing* clueless she was about their culture.

"You? Dangerous?"

She laughed, but the sound was a little unsure, her eyes wide and wary as she watched his every movement. As expected, there was the little flicker downward of her gaze to his scars for a second, but then she fixed her eyes resolutely on his, as though by ignoring his scars they didn't exist.

"You're not dangerous, to me..." She cleared her throat, a small cough to cover her unease. "Not to any of us. You said it yourself, we're under your protection and that of the emperor..."

Oh goddess, she really was clueless. Laarn bit back a growl as he started to advance. She really needed to be taught a lesson if she thought any Lathar warrior was harmless.

"Not dangerous?" he asked, his voice light as he stalked forward. Her survival instincts must have kicked in because she backed up, keeping the diagnostic bed between them like a shield. "Sure about that?"

"Uh-huh." She nodded, but he could see the tremor that rolled through her tiny frame. Lust flared to life within him, his cock rock hard in an instant and ready to burst through his leathers. It had been a long time since he'd had a woman, a long time since *any* woman had interested him. But *she* did.

All he could think of was pinning her against one of the beds, boosting her up onto its large flat surface, and what she'd look like beneath him, her hair spread out around her head like a dark cloud. The mental image brought a growl to his throat, and he stalked her around the bed.

"Laarn?"

Her voice was breathy. Soft. He could almost

imagine what she'd sound like if she moaned. It didn't help the state of his body any and his cock jerked savagely. He was hard enough to punch through steel, never mind through the well-worn warrior's leathers he wore beneath his healer's sash.

She circled the bed again, but he was ready for her. Instead of going around it, he planted a hand in the center and vaulted over to land on her side. Her little gasp fed his arousal further, and she backed up with her hands out as if to ward him off.

"Still think I'm not dangerous?" He couldn't help taunting her, each stalking step forward slow and deliberate. "Think again. *Every* warrior is dangerous. Especially to you. *Every* warrior out there has spent a lifetime without a woman… Only the oonat." He curled his lip in disgust. "*Animals.* Some of us won't touch them… Meaning there are men out there who have spent a lifetime without knowing the soft touch of a woman, having felt delicate skin under a calloused palm, or the scent of her skin wrapping around his will like a siren's call."

Her eyes widened as each of his descriptions matched a further step back until her back hit the wall between two support struts. He reached them, planting his hands either side of her head so she was corralled. Captive. At his mercy.

Just where he wanted her.

"And with men like that around," he continued, knowing he was talking about himself as much as any of them. "Men half-crazy with lust and hunger, you still think it's a good idea to walk around alone? Unprotected? Unguarded?"

He inched forward with each word, until he pressed against her, her breasts flush with his broad chest. This close, he could see the flutter of her pulse at her throat, fast and wild... the shortness of her breath as she struggled to breathe, and the darkening of her eyes as she looked up at him.

He had to be scaring her, but he didn't care. She needed to know this. She needed to be scared, to be wary of any warrior. And who better to give her the lesson than a scarred monstrosity like him. A man she was already terrified of... and couldn't bear to look at. Scaring her sent a lance of pain through his heart, but he steeled himself against it. Better him than another warrior. Any other warrior wouldn't just scare her to make a point, he'd claim her, bind her to him, and then she would have no escape.

Just as he wanted to... He fought that thought down, locking it away in the back of his mind. He wouldn't claim her, couldn't claim her because there was no way she would want him to. So he'd stick to just scaring her into being more sensible. Or, goddess help him, he'd kill any warrior who claimed her when she didn't want them to.

*What happens when she **does** want them to?* The little voice in the back of his head wanted to know. He ignored that as well, not even wanting to think along those lines. He would deal with it when it happened.

"I'm not unguarded. You're here to protect me," she argued, her hands on his broad chest as she tried to push against him.

The warning growl from the back of his throat put a stop to that and she looked up at him with wide eyes. They were the clearest blue, pale and piercing, and haunted his dreams. The round shape, so unlike his own slitted pupils, fascinated him.

"Perhaps I don't want to protect you."

His voice was blunt and rough as he slid a hand into her hair, cupping the back of her neck and hauling her up against him. He expected her to struggle, steeled his hold against it as he covered her lips with his. Hard and ruthless, he swept a tongue against her lips, prying them open to delve inside.

But she didn't struggle. Her lips parted as she melted against him. Her sweet taste exploded on his tongue, the softness he found almost bringing him to his end then and there. Soft hands went from pushing him to clinging, and then one of them slid up into his hair. Another growl broke from the back of his throat as her slender fingers tangled in the long locks, teasing and tempting him.

It was just too much. He'd intended the kiss to be a warning, nothing more, nothing less. But feeling her surrender against him, her mouth soft and pliant under his kiss, as her curvy little body was submissive against his was just too much. Sliding his hands down her sides, he ducked down and hoisted her up to pin her against the wall with his body, wrapping her legs around his hips.

She whimpered under his lips and the tiny noise sent arousal thundering though his veins like a *drakeen* tank-bot on a charge. His kiss turned from hard and brutal to slow and sensual. Expecting her to push him away at any moment, he concentrated on memorizing the taste of her, how she felt under his hands, the feeling of her hands in his hair. If he never had another taste of heaven like this, he wanted to remember every moment.

But she didn't push him away. Instead, her hips rocked against his and he groaned, his cock hard and heavy against the warmth of her covered pussy. His hands tightened on her hips and it was all he could do to keep them there. The long skirts of her robe swirled around them, trapped between them, but they were nothing more than a flimsy barrier. It would be the work of a moment to tear the delicate fabric from her, rip open his leathers and bury himself balls deep in her softness. Claim her as his own.

And she would hate him for it. She couldn't even look at him.

Pulling away, he ignored her little sound of disappointment with iron control and looked down at her with a hard look.

"See how easy it would be for me to take you?" he bit out, hands turning hard on her hips, holding her still before he lost all sense or reason. "I could easily tear this pretty little thing from you and fuck you senseless up against this wall, and there's nothing you could do to stop me. *Nothing,*" he growled, shaking her slightly when she opened her mouth to speak. A roll of his hips had his cock pressing hard against her.

"I could take you, use you any way I wanted to, and there would be nothing, *nothing,* you could do about it. You think all warriors are like Tarrick and Karryl?" He laughed harshly. "We're not. They're the good guys. You get that? They're both honorable and *nice.* I'm not. Not many of us are. You understand me?"

Her eyes widened, fear finally sneaking into the blue, and she nodded. Hating himself for putting it there, he let go of her and set her on her feet. "You're lucky I came along to save you from Saal J'Qess," he rumbled as he stepped away, trying to ignore the fact she was unsteady on her feet as she straightened her dress. "He's an asshole. I've heard him boasting about his exploits. He'd claim you and keep you on your knees, your mouth, pussy or ass filled with cock."

Just the thought of her in the other warrior's bed was enough to send fury ripping through him. Quickly, he turned away so she wouldn't see his expression, the need and lust he knew had to be written on his features. She wasn't for him, no matter what his uncle said, and the quicker he got that through his head the better.

"Right, since you're here," he grumbled. "We might as well make use of the time. I have extra tests I can run, and then I'll take you back to the women's quarters."

3

Three days later Jess' lips still tingled from Laarn's kiss. He'd barely looked at her as he'd run a barrage of tests, ignoring the few questions she'd gotten up the courage to ask. Her body had been on fire for his touch, but once he'd let her go, it had been as though she hadn't existed as a woman.

Again.

Frustration beat at her as she paced in the central room of the women's quarters, a common feeling where the tall, handsome healer was concerned. Her steps took her across the plush run in the middle of the floor and back again, the soft swish of her skirts against her ankles a calming refrain completely ignored in her agitation.

He'd kissed the daylights out of her, giving her a hint of the kind of passion she'd only dreamed of before he shut her out. Stopping at the window, she looked out over the courtyard below. A number of the K'Vass warriors were training down there and she absently watched them, admiring the strength and speed they moved with and the power in their big, masculine bodies. The fact that they were related to her on a species level still boggled her mind. How had they gotten from the lethal grace and sheer size of the Lathar to humanity?

"They're amazing. Aren't they?" Kenna's voice sounded by her ear as the other woman came to stand beside her. "Utterly amazing in a firefight. Have you seen them training with the combat bots yet?"

Jess shivered, remembering the attack and subsequent capture of the sentinel base where all the women had been captured. They'd used the red-eyed, silver-skinned bots then. Their bladed fingers still gave her nightmares. "No, not yet. I hate those things."

Thankfully, there weren't many of them in the Imperial palace, within the walls anyway. It seemed that for anything other than exterior defense, the

Lathar preferred "real" guards. Warriors guarded the corridors and halls in pairs.

"Oh, they're not that bad." Kenna moved forward, cocking up a hip and perching on the edge of the wide windowsill, the better to watch the warriors training below. "You should see the bigger bots, the *drakeen*. They're awesome."

Jess watched the other woman's gaze search through the big fight happening in the middle of the training area. It looked like a bloody and brutal free-for-all, but within a minute, there was a roar and a warrior emerged from the bottom of the pile, shedding the others like a dog shook water off its coat.

Xaandril, the emperor's champion, was instantly recognizable with his short, silver-blond hair and the tattoo-like marks all over his body.

Kenna breathed a sigh of relief and then caught herself, glancing quickly at Jess as if to see if she'd noticed. Jess hid her small smile and kept the neutral look on her face.

"He's a big guy," she commented, noncommittally. "Not sure many warriors could take him on. Good job he's not shown an interest in any of us," she couldn't help adding, just to see if she got a reaction. She did. A flush spread over Kenna's high cheekbones.

"He lost his wife and daughter apparently." The former marine's voice was softer than usual. "I don't think he's interested in trying again."

Jess had been about to answer that she didn't think that was the case when a chirp from the other room drew her attention. The sound announced an incoming communication, and it was coming from her room.

She frowned. The only people who knew where to reach her were Terran Command and her family. Command usually contacted either Jane, since as a major, she was the highest ranking among them, or Cat, who, thanks to her marriage to Tarrick, was technically a Latharian princess now.

"Sorry, I just need to get that," she called over her shoulder as she headed for her room.

All the rooms branched off the central area, and they were all the same. Large with high-vaulted ceilings, they were all decorated in the marble and white color scheme of the rest of the palace with gauzy drapes at the windows. Despite the elegant opulence, the windows were some sort of blast, laser and bullet-proof glass to match the heavy-duty defense shutters that could be rolled down over the doors at the touch of a button—all for the protection of the human women within.

Some among the Lathar hadn't rejoiced at the discovery of what at first had been hailed as a genetically compatible species, dismissing them as sub-Lathar in disgust. They'd insisted that breeding with humanity would corrupt what was left of the Lathar gene pool and lead to the destruction of their race.

There had been several attacks, the most prominent at Cat and Tarrick's wedding. But there had apparently been more after, leading to Daaynal installing the heavy-duty security to protect the unmated human women since they didn't have mates to ensure their safety.

The chirp from the comms console in the corner grew more agitated as she crossed the room. "Okay, okay, keep your bloody hair on," she grumbled as she slid into the soft seat in front of it.

She hit the answer button and smiled when her mother's face appeared on screen. Almost instantly the expression faltered as she registered the worried expression and the tears in her mother's eyes.

"Mom? Oh my god, what happened?"

Amanda Kallson wasn't normally an emotional woman—bringing up three children on her own had seen to that—but now her emotions were written all over her face.

"It's Lizzie, Jess," she managed to get out, tears streaming down her face. "She's ill, really ill."

The words stopped Jess in her tracks, the world... hell, the universe freezing around her. Her twin, Lizzie, had been there all her life since they'd shared a womb together, and although she was the homebody to Jess' adventurer, the thought of her twin being ill... or worse... ripped a hole right through her heart.

"Mom, calm down. What's happened?"

Only her military training allowed Jess to sit there calmly, her voice soothing as she tried to calm her tearful mother down. A chill crawled up her spine as her mom took a shaky breath and wiped her eyes. The tears still cascaded down her cheeks.

"She's been sick for a while. We thought at first it was just a cold... you know we had the arborian flu through here a couple of months back? Well, some people had relapses, so we thought it might just be that."

Jess nodded. While not usually lethal, arborian

flu was a nasty son of a bitch, liable to come back for a second or third bite after the initial infection. And, unusually, it didn't target the elderly or the weak, but young and healthy people like Lizzie and Jess.

"B-but then she didn't recover. She got weaker... she didn't want us to tell you since you're... well, *there.*" Amanda flicked a wide-eyed glance over Jess' shoulder as though she expected a horde of alien warriors to storm in and snatch Jess away right in front of her eyes.

"She wouldn't let us take her to the medical center, said it was just a bug that would pass." Amanda's voice broke, her face creased with pain. "But she went into the shower last night and collapsed in the stall. She's in a coma. The doctors don't know what's wrong with her. Jess... please, come home. I'm scared we're going to lose her."

"I NEED to see the emperor. Please!" Jess begged the stony-faced guard who had blocked access to the Imperial war-room where Daaynal was supposed to be. "It's a matter of life and death."

"The emperor is in a meeting with his advisors

and cannot be disturbed." The guard's face was hard, no give at all in his expression. "I will ensure he gets your message. If he deems it worthy of note, he will get back to you."

"You don't *understand!*" She blinked back tears, knowing that a show of emotion here would get her nowhere with the stony-faced guard. "It concerns Earth—" Okay, so maybe that was a stretch but she didn't care. She had to get to Daaynal, and get him to agree to send her home. "I had a communication from home that he needs to know about."

The guard simply looked down his nose at her. "The emperor will contact you if he wishes. Now, please, move along before I have to remove you from the room."

For a split second, Jess stood her ground. Perhaps if she did kick off and cause a scene, the commotion would reach Daaynal in the rooms off the war-room and he'd come to investigate.

"That won't be necessary," a deep male voice announced behind her. She turned with a small gasp to find Saal behind her, his big frame taut with tension and his expression hard as he walked toward her. His attention wasn't on her, though, but on the guard.

"I'll ensure the Lady Jessica gets back to the

women's quarters. She won't bother you further." As he spoke, he took hold of her arm and pulled her away to march her across the big room.

"What the hell do you think you're doing, Saal?" she hissed, trying to free herself from his hold.

His grip was firm though, unbreakable, as he slid her a sideways look. "Keep walking," he warned, a new tone in his voice. "Dvarr is a purist. You really don't want to provoke him or end up at his mercy. Trust me."

She gasped, about to turn and look back toward the asshole guard, but Saal swept her out into the corridor before she could.

"A purist? One of those assholes who attacked Cat and Tarrick's wedding? Are you sure?" she demanded, looking up at him as he stopped. Instead of trying to crowd her against the wall as he always had before, he let go of her arm and stepped back. "How do you know?"

He shrugged, his leather jacket pulling across his broad shoulders. "I hear things, rumors and gossip. Not everyone is happy about having humans here, or happy that you're being kept away from most of us. Most of us just want a fair chance at claiming one of you, but Dvarr isn't one of them. He and warriors like him would happily wipe you from existence to avoid 'tainting' our bloodlines."

"But... that's crazy." She shook her head in disbelief. "You guys have no women. No women, no bloodlines. Someone should explain the birds and the bees to him."

"The what and the what?" The big warrior looked confused. "Never mind. What was so important that you decided to go toe to toe with an Imperial guard?"

She couldn't help it. Far from being an asshole, Saal actually seemed concerned about her. The change threw her and brought tears back to her eyes.

"I need to go home. My sister is sick, like *really* sick. I need to go be with her before..."

She couldn't finish the sentence, the unthinkable stealing her ability to form thoughts, let alone shape them into words.

"Oh goddess... I'm sorry," he murmured in a deep voice and made a move to step forward. At the last moment, he stopped, his hands out to the sides to show he wasn't going to touch her although she read the desire too plainly and clearly in his eyes. "Are you close?"

She nodded, pulling a tissue from her sleeve to

wipe at her eyes. "She's my twin... my *litaan,*" she corrected.

His expression cleared, his eyes wide at the Latharian word for twin. "Humans have *litaan*-female births?" he asked in surprise.

"Yeah. It's as common as twin males and male-female twins." It was her turn to frown in confusion. "Why?"

He shrugged. "I've never heard of it before. Lathar *litaan* are usually male, or rarely a male and female pair are born. I can understand now, though, why you need to go home."

"But I can't see Daaynal, so I can't!"

She bit her lip in frustration, letting Saal guide her down the corridors back toward the women's quarters. Any ulterior motive she'd felt from him before had disappeared after his unexpected gallantry in saving her from Dvarr's threat.

Saal stopped, the doors to the women's quarters in sight, his hand on her arm. She started at the unexpected contact, but he didn't try to keep a hold on her. He just stopped her and then removed his hand.

"Listen," he said in a low voice, checking up and down the corridor to make sure no one was listening. "If you need to go home, I have a ship..."

She cut him a sideways look of surprise. "We're under the protection of the emperor. Wouldn't that get you into trouble?"

He shrugged. "Probably, but for you I would."

Jess backed off a step, searching his face. "Are you saying…"

His next words confirmed her suspicion. "I have a ship. Accept my claim and I'll take you home."

HAVING Jess in his arms had rocked him to the soul. Her soft curves against him, the silk of her hair over his hands, the sweet sound of her surrender under his lips as he claimed her mouth. Laarn growled, his palms flat against the cool surface of the counter in front of him as his cock gave a savage ache, not at all happy, even days later, that he hadn't claimed her as his own.

He could have. She was warm and willing, soft and open to him. It would have been the work of a moment to tear her dress from her body and impale her on his cock. Then he'd have had her for always, in his life. In his bed…

And, *lady,* did he want that.

Keeping his eyes closed, he fought to get himself

under control. Luckily, the lab was empty, as per his instructions. Since the kiss incident he'd given orders he was working alone, researching the disease that was killing their race. It wasn't unusual for him to do so. He often shut himself away when he was working on a problem—be it a complex new surgery, treatment plans for a large-scale virus, or this, the most important medical issue that the Lathar had ever faced.

The medical staff were used to it. Apart from leaving meals by the door of his lab, they mainly left him alone, paging him if he was needed in the main med-bay. So far, they'd only had to do it once, when a warrior had required extensive spinal surgery after a training accident. The male had been cleaved almost in two, his ribs detached from his spine on one side and the body cavity open.

The fact he'd made it to surgery was testament to the hardiness of their race, but it had meant Laarn had a twelve-hour fight himself as he battled time and nerve damage to put the warrior back together. He'd done it. He wasn't lord healer for nothing. Complex surgery for battle wounds was one of his specialties.

As was genetic manipulation, a requirement for even *thinking* about ascension to the lord healer position. The Lathar as a race had been extensively genetically modified over their history, to better adapt them for combat and various other reasons. The exploration team that had eventually become the human race, for example, had been modified to be smaller and reproduce prolifically. Further evidence they had been intended for eventual colonization. Where along the way their eyes had changed, he didn't know.

A chirp brought his head up sharply. The holographic display over the main desk in front of him was brightly lit, displaying the results of one of the many tests he was running simultaneously and continuously, trying to figure out how to fix the damage to the Latharian genetic code. There was a pulsing light in one of the sectors, indicating that one of the tests had reached its conclusion.

He frowned as he straightened up, tucking his hair behind his ears as he pulled the information from the edge of the screen into the middle of the display. A flick and spread of his fingers opened the data file, and the information rolled out before his eyes.

Which widened. The test was one of the investigatory ones he'd instigated on the DNA of their human guests when they'd arrived—mapping and exploring the new genetic information. The task had become even more important once he'd realized that the similarities between them as species weren't random... that they were related. Even altered Latharian DNA might hold clues to help him in his task.

As he read the results, his eyes narrowed, his agile mind working over the data and fitting it in with what he already knew. From the look of it, the exploration group that had become the Terrans had left the Lathar before other genetic manipulations had been made. Excitement rose in his chest.

If they had, that explained the lack of slitted pupils, a manipulation that had been made eons ago to adapt the Lathar for fighting in planetary systems with high levels of light in the artorian spectrum. But it also meant their core genetic information might contain information long since lost from the Lathar code.

Leaning forward, his hands moved swiftly over the holographic display, flicking and pinching in midair as he worked his way through the results with a fervor that burned in his chest. His breathing shortened and his body was tight with tension as his big heart pounded. The information he sought was here. He just knew it was. All he had to do was find it.

The universe narrowed down to two things. His gaze zeroed in on what he was reading and his hands as he cut through useless data to find what he needed. Then, in one perfect moment, he spotted it. There was a strand of data he'd almost missed, hidden behind another, and he almost scrolled past it. At the last moment though, his brain kicked him in the ass and he rolled back, stabbing the data-stream with a finger and then flicking it wide to expand it onto his screen.

His breathing all but stopped as the code rolled out. Then excitement burst through him with all the force and brilliance of a supernova. There it was—a pure, unaltered snippet of DNA. He'd never seen it before, never once in the altered and hacked about code he'd been seeing all his life, but its purity shone through like the lady goddess herself.

That was it. That was the answer he'd been looking for. His hands moving over the holo-console at near light speed, he isolated the snippet, turning and manipulating it to fit into the Latharian genome.

"Holy shit..." he breathed as it locked into place, creating a bridge and strengthening several areas he hadn't even realized were a problem. The change caused a chain reaction along the strand, fixing problems one by one until the helix glowed, perfectly healthy and rotating in front of his eyes.

The smallest change, the tiniest snippet of code hidden in the background that, at some point, had been removed or corrupted in the code of the Lathar... and it was the key to everything. From a race some no longer considered Lathar. The humans.

More specifically, one of the human women. The self-same women they'd captured to slack their lust on had unwittingly provided the key to saving them as a race.

How fucking ironic.

"Who are you from?" He spoke to the glowing strand as if it were a person, a frown on his face as he dug deeper into the test results. They only had a few human women here, so whoever it belonged to was here, now. He could run further tests and save his people.

Isolating the sample the code had been extracted from, Laarn's heart about stopped as a name flashed across his screen.

Jessica Kallson, it read, followed by, *Human. Female. Captured by the Lathar from sector nine-seven-three-five-alpha.*

He rocked back on his heels.

His little Jessica was the female who would save them all.

Reaching his hand out, he triggered the comms system, opening a direct line to his uncle, the emperor. "Your Majesty, this is Laarn," he began. "I have results you're going to want to see."

4

It took Daaynal less than ten minutes to reach Laarn's lab, and the healer less than two to explain the situation. After studying the results for a long moment, Daaynal turned and Laarn found himself scrutinized by eyes so like his own.

"And you're sure?" the emperor asked, his expression serious.

Laarn nodded. "I've tested the patch myself several times and I have the healer's hall AI on it, testing out every variant I can think of and probably a million I can't."

The emperor nodded, his expression thoughtful. One hip leaning back against the edge of the console, he studied the data scrolling over the screen in front of them. Even though he wasn't a trained healer, Laarn wouldn't have been surprised in the least if he understood most of it.

Daaynal liked to present himself as the big, dumb warrior, complete with leathers and braids, but it was all an act. The male had a mind like a steel trap, could pilot not only one but multiple *drakeen* at the same time, and his *litaan* had been a mathematical genius who had written most of the base programming for the AIs in use across the empire.

"And the human female, Jessica, is the key?" he asked, proving Laarn's unspoken theory that he understood the information on the screen by stepping forward and pulling up her records.

The display changed to show Jess' picture on one side. It was the one taken when they'd processed her aboard the *Velu-vias* just after she'd been captured. Laarn's heart clenched at the sight. She looked scared, her dark hair mussed and dirt on her cheek. Her biological information flowed over the section of screen below the picture but he ignored it—he knew it by heart—as Daaynal pulled up the section of code Laarn had found hidden in her DNA.

"This is it?" he asked. "And she's the only one of the females who has it?"

"Yes and yes," Laarn confirmed. "It's the tiniest portion of information, but one that was deleted from our own code eons ago. I think, and this is just a theory at the moment, that it was an anchor point. With it gone, our genome gradually degraded and started to come apart, to the point we are now. As such, it's only going to get worse. Soon we'll lose the ability to procreate at all. Then we'll see the sickness extended to adult males as it did with adult females in the last generation."

Silence fell between the men for a long moment. Both remembered the plagues that swept their society, their women dying from stupid small illnesses in swathes, with no cause they could identify until they'd looked deeper.

Daaynal shuddered, but his voice was hard. Determined.

"No. The empire will not fall on my watch."

Turning, he looked directly at Laarn. Gone was the amiable uncle he'd been talking to, and in his place was the emperor of the Lathar.

"Do what you need to do. *Whatever* you need to do," he ordered. "Jessica Kallson does not leave this planet. Find others with this genetic information in the Terran prisoners we have. If you can't, we'll find them on Earth. Their defenses are pitiful. It won't take long to break the planet."

Just like that, the human women went from being honored guests to prisoners again.

"Yes, Your Majesty." Laarn bit back a twinge of guilt that he'd been the one to spark the change, but he straightened his spine with resolve. He was first and foremost Lathar. If humanity offered the key to their salvation, they had to take it, even if it meant subjugating an entire subspecies. "I'll order the remaining females tested and bring Jess back in for more tests."

The emperor nodded, arms folded across his big chest. "I suggest you claim this particular human female," he said abruptly, his focus fixed on Laarn's face. "If I'm reading your research right, she would be the best candidate for a pregnancy, would she not?"

Shit. He hadn't seen that one coming. Suddenly wary, Laarn nodded slowly.

Daaynal smiled, the expression feral and predatory. "Good. Then that child, the savior of our race, *will* be from our bloodline. Claim the woman and get her pregnant. As soon as possible."

Laarn opened his mouth to argue. A myriad of reasons screamed that wasn't a good idea. She was human, and tiny... he'd already scared her half to death and that was before taking into account she would barely look at him because of his scars. He was a monster to her.

But... the little voice in the back of his head murmured seductively, *she surrendered to you, was soft and pliant in your arms. She didn't scream or fight when you nearly claimed her against the wall...*

"Do it." Daaynal's voice was as hard as a whip and colder than the frozen wastes of *Telu-noresh,* his expression harder. "Or I will."

"No? What do you mean, no?"

Jess felt like she'd been pole-axed as she stood in front of Daaynal, looking up into an expression that lacked the normal warmth and smile she was used to seeing on the big emperor's face. Now his expression was closed off and forbidding as he lounged on the throne, green eyes so like Laarn's boring into hers.

"Have a care, little human," he rumbled, an edge of anger in his deep voice. "That you do not overstep your bounds as my *guest.*"

She shivered at the note in the last word, all her

illusions about her place at court stripped away in one spine-chilling moment. He'd lauded Jess and her companions as honored guests but the Lathar were ruthless. It seemed as soon as having them as guests was no longer useful, they'd be downgraded back to the prisoners they'd started out as.

Straightening her spine, she nodded. Something had happened to change the status-quo but she wasn't sure what. There was no way she was asking him either. Just one look at his demeanor and she knew he wasn't going to say anything. The emperor did not explain himself. Ever.

"My apologies, Your Majesty," she murmured with a small curtsy. "I meant no offense."

Her words were calm, but inside she screamed with frustration. The need to get home, to see her twin, was all she could think about.

"It's just my sister is very ill. My mother says she's getting worse."

Daaynal didn't move, still leaning back in his chair, chin propped on long fingers. "Be that as it may, the journey back to Terra is long and fraught with dangers. It would be remiss of me as your protector to allow you to undertake such a hazardous journey."

"B..." She took a breath, schooling her response

as she tried another avenue. "But surely with the reputation the Lathar enjoy, deservedly so, within the universe as premier warriors... no one would dare attack one of your ships? Unless of course you intend for me to make the journey back alone?"

How she'd do that she had no idea. She and the rest of the women had been taken from the sentinel base aboard Tarrick's ship, any human ships destroyed in the attack. There was nothing here from Earth she could make a return trip in.

"Indeed, however I have nothing free that I can assign to you, not with the problems in the Rivaas sector. I might consider it in a cycle or so when the situation there becomes clearer."

Tears burning the backs of her eyes, Jess nodded, remembering to curtsy again. "Yes, Your Majesty, thank you."

Daaynal inclined his head, his gaze flicking over her shoulder for a moment. The ghost of a smile crossed his features but she didn't think much of it. She'd thought he was an okay guy, but it turned out he was as ruthless as his reputation had suggested. More fool her. She should have known that just because he looked like a human didn't mean he had the same morals and values.

A gentle breeze fluttered the drapes at the

windows, bringing the scent of the flowers from the gardens beyond into the room. The light scent would have made her smile before but right now, she couldn't muster it.

"With your permission, Your Majesty?" she murmured with a curtsy, both signaling her intention to leave and requesting permission at the same time. Normally Daaynal just nodded or waved a hand indicating she could, but this time he looked directly at her.

"A moment, Ms. Kallson. I believe my nephew has need of you."

"He does?" Jess turned with a frown, expecting to find Tarrick behind her. Instead, she came face to face with Laarn, his green eyes piercing as he looked down at her. After their kiss, she'd expected to go beet-red when she saw him again, but thanks to the emotions churning in her stomach because of her sister, she gave him a small nod, her ability to process new emotions frozen.

"Lord Healer," she nodded to acknowledge him, using the term of address she'd heard some of the warriors use around him. "How can I help you?"

His expression shifted, the tiniest hint of a frown crossing his brow. "Lord Healer?" he asked. "What happened to using my name? I thought we were friends, Jessica?"

She lifted a shoulder slightly, keeping her expression level and neutral. Friends didn't kiss each other like he'd kissed her the other day, enfolding her in his strong arms and enticing her with kisses full of dominance and passion. But that had been before she'd found out about Lizzie.

"So did I," she said quietly, unable to keep the bitter little note out of her voice no matter how hard she tried. "The same as I bought the line that we were guests rather than prisoners here. Funny how wrong I was."

JESS WAS UPSET. More upset than he'd ever seen her. Admittedly, he hadn't known her that long—it had only been a little over two months since they'd first discovered the existence of the humans in their little backwater systems—but in that time he'd been closely observing the human women, their manners and behaviors as well as their moods and emotions. He'd seen them scared, defiant, angry, amused, happy...

Jess was none of those things. Her shoulders

were tight as she walked beside him toward his lab. Her lips were set in a pursed line and, as he cut a sideways glance down at her beautiful face, he swore he saw tears glinting in the corners of her eyes.

The sight made his heart ache, her closed off mood affecting him more than he cared to admit. What was it about one tiny human female that could affect him so much? He was a warrior of the Lathar. *He* controlled his emotions, not the other way around.

As much as he told himself that, it made no difference. As soon as they stepped into his lab and the doors closed behind them, he stopped her with a big hand on her arm.

"Jessica. What's wrong? Did someone hurt you?"

She looked at his hand and instantly he removed it. A warrior didn't seek to touch a female he didn't intend to claim, not without good reason and never for long. To do otherwise was without honor. Now he had her attention, he had no reason to touch her further, even though every cell in his body urged him to step forward and take her into his arms.

The face she turned up to him was calm and composed, but the pain in her eyes almost brought him to his knees.

"My sister is sick," she said softly. "I need to go

home, but Daaynal won't let me. She could die and I won't be there." Before the end of the sentence, a lone tear detached itself from the corner of her eye and slid down her cheek.

Before he knew what he was doing, Laarn stepped forward, wrapping his arms around her small form and pulling her against him. She froze, stiff for a moment, but then relaxed against him, the sound of her soft sobs filling the silence of the lab.

"Shhh, shhh..." he whispered, his lips against her hair. "It will be okay. Your sister won't die." He didn't know that for sure, but he didn't care. He'd promise anything just to take that note of pain out of her voice.

Falling silent, she nodded, her face buried against his chest. He tightened his arms, liking the feeling of her resting against him so trustingly. Guilt stabbed through him.

If she knew what he'd been ordered to do, claim her and get her pregnant regardless of any feelings she had on the matter, she wouldn't cling to him quite so readily. Not if she knew she was a hairsbreadth away from being bonded to him for life.

His mood took a nosedive, his jaw tightening until he could feel a muscle at the side jumping. No matter what his uncle said about claiming her, he couldn't. She couldn't even look at him without his jacket on... there was no way she'd want to spend a lifetime with him.

No, better they avoid that. The little plan that had been formulating in the back of his mind took root and began to grow. All he needed was to confirm that Jess could get pregnant, and that the unaltered sequence in her DNA meant what he thought it meant—that she could conceive a female child, the first female Lathar born for decades. She didn't need to actually *get* pregnant... all he needed was to confirm it in the lab.

"It will all be fine." He smoothed a hand down her back, trying hard not to think about how good she felt in his arms and how perfectly she fit there. "I'll talk to my uncle, see if I can get him to see sense."

"Oh, would you?" she gasped, leaning back to look up at him. Her eyes were wet with tears, but the redness there didn't detract from her beauty in any way. The hope in her eyes hit him in the gut, but that was nothing to when she reached up on her toes and kissed his cheek quickly.

"Bless you. Thank you so much. It would mean so much to me. Lizzie and I... well, there's never been a me without her. To hear that she's sick..." She shrugged. "I'm terrified I'll lose her before I see her again."

He frowned, looking down at her as he made sense of what she said. Thanks to the translation implants, he understood Terran. But sometimes *how* they said things completely baffled him and he had to think about it to decode it.

"What do you mean, there's never been a you without your sister?" His expression cleared. "Do you mean you were born at the same time? That's not possible unless you're—"

"Twins, yes." She nodded, smiling at his obvious confusion. "Lizzie is my *litaan*. Apparently, you don't have female twins in the Lathar?"

"No." Lady goddess, that was it. Realization hit him like a ship at light speed. The bridge code in her DNA was because she was a *litaan*. It was the only explanation.

"No, we don't. Lady goddess, that might be useful. Can I..." he gestured toward the big diagnostic bed behind her. "Could I run a few more tests with that in mind? It might help to cross reference your DNA with the records of other *litaan* in our database. We have male-female pairs and male-male pairs but as far as I know we have never had a female-female pair. If humans do, that makes me wonder why."

"Of course, anything that will help," she said, easing from his arms and approaching the bed.

She stopped and, for a moment, his attention hijacked by the delicate curve of her neck revealed by her up-swept hair, he wondered why. Then he realized the bed was too high. Usually he made sure it was set on the lowest level, one that was easy for the much smaller human women to boost themselves up onto, but his last patient had been one of the bigger warriors, so it was still set near the maximum height.

"Here, let me help you," he murmured, reaching her side in a couple of strides. Normally he'd have reached out and adjusted the height on the side with a wave of his hand, but he didn't. Instead, he stepped in, big hands on either side of her tiny waist and simply lifted her onto the bed.

Once he had her there, though, he couldn't make his hands let go. They remained locked around her tiny waist. She looked up at him, a frown on her beautiful face. He couldn't do it, couldn't let her go despite all the reasons saying he should.

"Laarn?"

His name on her lips was little more than a

whisper, but he heard it. All sense abandoning him, he stepped forward, using his hip to push her thighs apart so he could step between them. Her breathing caught, a little hitch that did all kinds of things to his body that should be illegal, and her eyes widened.

A big hand on the back of her hips and he pulled her up flush against him. His cock, hard, heavy and almost busting the seams of his leathers, pressed insistently against her pussy. Her eyes darkened, and the tiniest moan sounded in the back of her throat.

He answered it with a low growl, free hand latching at the back of her neck as he tilted her head up to the perfect angle.

"Forgive me," he murmured against her lips a moment before he claimed them.

His kiss was hard and unforgiving, less a kiss and more a punishment to himself for not having better self-control. For losing it the instant he touched her. He punished them both by deepening the kiss immediately, prying her lips apart to taste the sweetness within. His tongue slid against hers, not stroking gently but demanding her response.

It wasn't enough. Would never be enough. His hand in her hair tightened, and she whimpered against him, her own hands digging into the broadness of his shoulders. The sound brought him back to his senses a little, and he gentled his kiss just enough that her hands relaxed against him. No longer claws against pain, but touching him, stroking him. Teasing him in her own way.

Surprise washing through him, he eased up a little more and slid the hand on the back of her hips further up—a softer touch than he thought he was capable of. Than he *should* be capable of. A warrior born and bred, even with his healer's training, he'd never be a gentle man. But for her he wanted to be, for her... He'd be anything she needed.

His tongue stroked against hers, and he growled in need as his cock jerked and pulsed. Just one little push. That's all it would take, and she could be beneath him on the bed, her hair spread out around her head just like in his daydreams.

But then he felt her hands at the fastening to his jacket. Ice washed through his veins and he froze. Without being conscious of the movement, he clamped a hard hand over both of hers, stopping her undoing the garment. He wanted nothing more than to feel her hands on him, to feel her soft fingers exploring his body, but it wouldn't happen. As soon as she felt his skin, she'd recoil and push him away.

It had happened before. He always had to pay extra at any of the pleasure houses for them to touch him, to suffer touching his marked body, and even then none of them had been able to keep the revulsion out of their expressions. He didn't want to see that in Jess' eyes.

"No."

He disengaged himself, ignoring the howl of his male instincts and the savage jerk of his cock as it was denied the pleasure of sinking deeply into the haven of her pussy. The look she shot him, equal parts confusion and longing, almost broke his control but he stepped back, softening the rejection with a small smile.

"We have work to do," he reminded her gently, unable to resist reaching out to tuck a loose strand of hair behind her ear, his fingertips brushing her cheek before he dropped his hand. "The quicker we can do this, the quicker I can get to my uncle and persuade him to let you go home, okay?"

5

It was all Jess could do to nod slowly and not throw herself at Laarn as he pulled away. Again. Sexual frustration and confusion surged through her, the feeling so strong she wanted to scream. He wanted her, the hard length of his cock pressed against her pussy when he'd shoved his way between her legs had proven that... so why did he keep pulling away? What was the problem?

Realizing he was still looking at her for an answer, she took a deep breath and mustered a smile from somewhere. He'd touched her, voluntarily this time, the quick brush of his fingertips against her cheek leaving a trail of fire like a brand.

"If you'd just lie back for me."

His deep voice seemed rougher than normal as

he moved around the bed, the holographic display already starting up as she wriggled backward and pulled her legs up. By the time she lay back, it arched over her in a bridge of brightly colored light. She could see Laarn through it, his attention focused on the readouts, and she took the opportunity to study him without him noticing.

He was the most handsome man she'd ever seen, with strong features and long, dark hair. Filled with warrior's braids, it fell past his shoulders, not tied back like it usually was. Although he was identical in looks to his brother, Tarrick, she'd know the two men apart immediately, not only because Laarn's eyes were green, not gold, but because the way they moved was totally different. Laarn was more self-contained and reserved but with an edge of raw power and suppressed danger that hit her on a very primal level.

He frowned, his lips curling back a little in annoyance at something on the screen, and she couldn't help the slight smile. When he didn't know anyone was looking, his face was quite expressive. Right now, he looked frustrated as hell... it was cute, if a man his size could ever be called cute.

Allowing her gaze to wander over him, she studied the width of his shoulders and chest. Like the other warriors she'd seen, the fit of his jacket indicated he was packed with muscle, that impression backed by the solidity and power she'd felt under her hands a moment ago and the memories from the one time she'd seen him remove his shirt weeks ago.

His scars.

She blinked. He'd been all for kissing her, and more if the state of his body pressed against hers was any indication, until she'd tried to undo his jacket to touch him. Then he'd shut her down and stepped away so quickly her head had practically spun.

Oh shit... Could he be sensitive about his appearance?

Armed with this new possibility, she studied his face and hands again. With his jacket on, there was no evidence of the scars beneath, and he rarely took the jacket off around her or the other women, even though she knew his scars were like badges of honor in Latharian culture. Ones that proved just how good a doctor he was.

"It's warm in here, isn't it?" she started tentatively, wriggling a little on the bed. "Don't you get warm all dressed up like that?"

Okay, crude but it was all she could think of to start the conversation she wanted. He flicked a glance at her, the lights of the display highlighting his features and turning his eyes pale. She sucked a breath in, liking that he looked like a dark angel, ready to swoop in and ravish her.

His gaze flicked to the screen for a moment and his lips quirked. "I'm fine, but yes, your body temperature is slightly raised. I can drop the temperature on the bed to make you more comfortable."

She shivered as cool air washed over her. She hadn't meant that and from the quirk of his lips, he bloody well knew it.

"Okay..." His deep voice was almost back to normal as he stared intently at the screen in front of him. "I see the link to your *litaan*. There's some code here I haven't seen before. May I take some of your eggs to test a theory? Not many, I'll only harvest a few, and you won't feel a thing."

Jess paused, a frown between her brows. "Eggs? As in from my ovaries?"

He looked down at her through the display. A green light blinked on and off, reflected just under one eye. "Yes. From your ovaries, unless humans have a secondary location for them I know nothing about?"

"No." She shook her head. "It's the ovaries. But...

you'll only take a few, right? And I'll still be able to have kids? I...I'd like a baby someday. I don't want to lose that ability."

Instantly as she said it, she kicked herself. Crass thing to say to a man whose species struggled to reproduce. A flush on her cheeks, she tried to cover up her gaffe.

"I mean, with the right man... warrior... of course."

"You see yourself settling down with a warrior from my species?" he asked, his expression unreadable as his hands moved over the display in front of him. She had no clue how the medical machines worked, but she trusted him. If he said it wouldn't hurt, then it wouldn't. "Surely we seem a little... barbaric to you?"

She shrugged and then instantly grew still as he frowned and shook his head at her. Any answer she was going to give had to wait as the machine whirled colored lights around her, the intersecting lines speeding up as they focused on the area above her lower body. She tensed as warmth started to spread out from within her, but before she could fully analyze the feeling, it was gone and the lights clicked off.

"Was that it?" she asked in surprise, a small gasp

on her lips when he nodded. "I was expecting, I dunno... something more invasive. Like a big needle or something?"

Laarn chuckled, his darkly handsome face splitting into a wide grin. "Please, we may be barbaric in some aspects, but in medicine? I can assure you we are one of the most advanced races in the universe. Cellular translocation," he added, nodding toward her stomach. "I removed a couple of eggs, which I'll use for my tests. They'll be stored here in the lab rather than in medbay proper, so your genetic material isn't available to any of the other researchers. I appreciate your trust in me."

Something about the way he said it made her tilt her head to the side. Sitting up as the holo-arch shut down, she reached out to put her hand on his arm, speaking earnestly.

"I do trust you, Laarn, with my life. And I don't think you're barbaric..." She trailed off, her pointed look at him making it clear she might hold that view about the rest of his people, but that he was a different matter. "In fact, with the right man..." *Him.* "...the caveman act is rather hot."

"I'm telling you, I *need* access to the sister," Laarn argued, practically toe to toe with Daaynal just off the main training area.

Warriors around them pointedly looked the other way, apart from Karryl. His crossed arms and set expression said clearly he was prepared to back Laarn up, even against the emperor, but he expected they were both going to get a right pasting for it. Laarn made a mental note to thank his childhood friend later. No, they were more than that if he'd risk Daaynal's wrath for him. That made them brothers in arms, blood-brothers at the very least.

Daaynal's eyes, so like Laarn's own, widened.

"Oh, you do, do you?"

His chuckle was unexpected but welcome, a bolt of relief rolling through the healer. As big-built and accomplished among the warriors as Laarn was, Daaynal was both bigger and more experienced, the first warrior's braids in his hair years before Laarn and his brother had even been thought of. If he'd taken exception to Laarn's challenge, neither his relationship to the emperor nor his standing as the best healer in the empire would have saved him from a beating.

"Why... planning on claiming both of them for your own?" Daaynal crossed his arms, amusement washing over his features. Just off the training grounds, he sported a split lip and a freshly blacked eye that had yet to reach its full purple glory. A quick glance behind the warrior emperor revealed Xaandril training with his son, Rynn. No doubt the source of Daaynal's current injuries, he was obviously the recipient of some in return. Although he was covered in blood and held his left arm at an odd angle at his side, he was still more than capable of defending himself against his son... who appeared to be trying to kill him.

"I'm pretty sure there would be complaints if I allowed you to have two of the delightful creatures," Daaynal mused, rubbing at his stubbled chin with a big hand.

"No, *no*... I don't want two of them," he added hastily and then caught the glimmer of amusement in Daaynal's eyes, realizing he'd been had.

"Not two, but one at the least?" The emperor's grin broadened.

Laarn ignored him, carrying on talking. "I *do* need to check the sister's medical condition. Apparently, she's very ill and if she has the same genetic information as her sister—"

Daaynal frowned, the amusement gone as he pulled Laarn to one side away from the hustle and bustle of the training arenas into the shelter of the alcoves at the side of the palace.

"Why would she have the same genetic information? Is it possible she has the same bridge code as her sister?" Daaynal's expression sharpened at the possibility and Laarn nodded.

"More than possible given that they're *litaan.*" He paused to let that one sink in. "Apparently Terrans have female-female pairs, something we never have, not since antiquity. I've checked the other Terrans we have for the same code and none of them have it, not even the other female who reports she is also… a twin as the Terrans call them. Her *litaan* though is male, which leads me to think it's either solely in the female pair code, or… even rarer… it's solely in the DNA of the Kallson family."

"If it is… *Draanth…*" Daaynal breathed, running a hand through his hair and raking the loose strands from his face.

"Yeah… exactly. Can you see why I want to take Jess and secure her sister as well?" Laarn pushed, knowing how much getting back to Earth meant to his little Terran. Quite when she'd become *his* little Terran in his thoughts, he didn't know, and right at the moment it wasn't important.

Checking that the corridor running alongside

the alcoves was clear, he dropped his voice so that only his uncle could hear. "I managed to recover some of her eggs and tested my theory. Under lab conditions, pregnancy is possible. Of the eggs I tested, one is already a viable pregnancy."

Daaynal's eyes widened, a flash of something in the green depths. Satisfaction... hope maybe... or, and Laarn blinked at the thought, longing? He wasn't sure, and the quick flash was gone before he could analyze it.

"So you managed to adhere to my orders in your own unique way... *just,*" he chuckled, obviously amused. "A pregnancy without being pregnant. Unique. And possibly a safer alternative than having Miss Kallson actually be with child... especially with the current mood from certain elements of our society."

Laarn easily read the subtext. The purist idiots had been kicking up since the discovery of the Terrans in their little galaxy in the ass-end of beyond. They'd always had a hard-on against interbreeding with any species, even though with genetic manipulation, the females were only incubators for wholly Lathar offspring, but the arrival of the Terrans had kicked them into a frenzy. The clan leaders with purist tendencies had been very vocal about the Terrans and the threat of breeding with sub-Lathar species. If they got wind of an actual pregnancy, both mother and child would be in danger.

"Exactly. And that being said, surely you can see the reason I want a second test subject with that bridging code?" he pressed, feeling like a shit for hanging the threat of something happening to Jess over Daaynal's head.

Even as he said it, a hot surge of emotion and rage surged up from his soul. No one would hurt Jess. *Ever*. Not as long as he had breath left in his body. She was his to protect, and no one, especially not those bastard purists, would ever harm her.

Daaynal rubbed his chin again, eyes narrowed in assessment. "I can, but I can't allow you to take Ms. Kallson off planet. What happens if the ship you're on is attacked and the only female we have with the genetic code we need is killed? It's too great a risk."

Laarn sighed, frustration rolling through him. Daaynal had a point. Despite his feelings for Jess, he had to see the bigger picture. If they lost her before he could replicate the code and disseminate it through the population, they were back where they started, facing annihilation within a generation.

"But... It may be a suitable proving mission for a

younger warrior." The big emperor leaned back against the wall, his gaze not on Laarn but looking out over the training arena to where the Imperial champion and his son were still mid-battle. Laarn raised an eyebrow, surprised to see Rynn still on his feet and fighting. He must be as hard to kill as his sire.

"You'd have her brought here?" he asked, his tone carefully level. If he couldn't get Jess to Earth, bringing her ailing sister *here* where he could treat her was the next best thing.

"Yes. It seems the best solution all around." Daaynal pushed off from the wall with a grin. "It's decided then. Rynn will collect your woman's sister while I and his father decide how to deal with those asshole D'Farans on the outer borders who think I haven't noticed them building a small army out there."

"She's not my—" Laarn started automatically but then trailed off with a sigh as Daaynal swept away, issuing orders and stopping the fight between Xaandril and Rynn with a shout. His uncle seemed to have a mental block whenever he told him that Jess wasn't his.

Even though he wanted her to be...

6

"They're really pulling out all the stops, aren't they?" Jane asked with a grin, settling herself into the seat next to Jess in the covered pavilion that had been set up next to the warriors' arena.

It had been carefully cleared, the blood-stained sand removed and new sand carefully raked so the six challenge areas looked pristine. Seating had been placed all around the large rectangle, and long benches were interspersed with large seats for the clan leaders. Pride of place went to the raised and covered dais for the emperor, with the pavilion for the human women to one side as his honored guests.

"It seems that way, yes. Any idea what it's all in

aid of?" Jess asked, mustering a smile as she looked around. Guilt and frustration lay heavily on her. She should be going home, but since Daaynal had blown off her request yesterday, she hadn't been able to get an audience with him again. He mostly appeared to be busy between "Imperial duties" and whatever today was about.

"It's a tournament." Cat joined them in a swish of silken skirts. As the wife of an Imperial prince, she'd almost totally adopted Latharian clothing, a jeweled tiara nestled in her dark curls denoting her rank and status. "In our honor apparently. The warriors will compete against each other as a showcase of their abilities. Daaynal is offering a couple of ships to the overall winner."

"Shit, I should have entered myself. Just think what we all could do with a couple of Latharian ships..." Jane whistled softly.

With her marriage to a Lathar warrior, and her subsequent retirement from the Terran military, the former marine had also adopted Latharian dress. Instead of the silken robes and jewels Cat wore, though, Jane had gone for warrior's leathers, teamed with her own combat boots and a tank-top. Her dog tags were gone, replaced with a set of octagonal tags on a chain.

All the women wore them, Jess' own nestled next to her Terran dog tags, and they opened the weapons caches in the palace and on the ships of the K'Vass, as well as any of their allies. The Lathar had quickly realized that the human women they'd captured were not shrinking violets or damsels in distress. They'd all been personnel on a military base, so they knew one end of a rifle from the other, no matter what planet it had been manufactured on.

"Too right."

The last of their party, Kenna, joined them. Like Jane, she was a dyed in the wool marine, so she wore leathers with her combat boots and a leather bustier top that made the most of her ample bust. She caught Jess looking and winked. "Keeps their eyes off my hands, and the blaster at my hip. Surprisingly effective on any man, even a warrior born and bred, especially when they haven't seen proper women for decades..."

Jess chuckled. Trust Kenna. She was definitely the light relief in their party, and sometimes much needed. Before she could ask anything else, though, a fanfare sounded and the arena started to fill up. Warriors and robed and hooded figures, their courtesans, filled the seating around the main area, a sense of excitement filling the air. To their right, another fanfare rang out as Daaynal made his arrival. Instantly, the crowd were on their feet, shouting and cheering.

"The emperor hasn't called a tournament for years." Cat leaned forward so they could hear her. "It's only open to warriors above a certain ability level, so we're going to see the best of the best."

"Karryl's competing," Jane commented, a proud smile on her face as warriors began to enter the arena.

"Fellow warriors and honored guests!" Daaynal's voice rang out, cutting through the cheering of the crowd. "I bid you welcome to the first combat tournament on Lathar prime for decades. In times past, tournaments of this type were a common fixture at the palace, in the cities, right down to our villages... where the best warriors amongst us would compete to show off our skills and perhaps catch the eye of that special female to prove our worth as warrior and male. I do not need to remind you why such tournaments are no longer held." There was a moment's pause as his words sunk in, the enormity of the situation the Lathar as a species were in a sobering one.

Daaynal spoke again, sweeping his arm toward the sheltered pavilion the women sat in. "But... fate has smiled on us. Thanks to the discovery of the Terrans, a long-lost branch of the Lathar, we once again have the chance to show off our skills and abilities to worthy females."

He gestured to the silent warriors on the sand in front of him. "Before you, you see the best of our warriors. They will fight each other both together and solo until only one remains. The winner will become the proud owner of two of the empire's newest battlecruisers and, if he is lucky, may win the appreciation of one of our delightful ladies here today."

Kenna leaned forward, waggling her eyebrows. "I'd sure appreciate the hell out of half this lot. Have you seen the bodies on these guys?"

Jess bit back a small smile, easily seeing through Kenna's joking manner as she realized the other woman was doing exactly what she was—searching through the assembled men to find that one familiar figure. In Kenna's case, she stopped as soon as she found the tall, broad-shouldered figure of the emperor's champion, Xaandril, but Jess' eyes kept searching.

Laarn was a healer, so perhaps he wouldn't be here. She knew he trained, and could fight, but she wasn't sure if he was considered a warrior anymore or if his position as healer took precedence.

"And for the first time, I have a personal interest in the outcome of this tournament!" Daaynal announced, as a gong rang and two warriors walked out onto the sands, between the rows already assembled. "My sister-sons have taken to the sands, one a warrior prince and, for the first time in two generations, a lord healer."

The gasp that went around the crowd was echoed by Cat. "Shit," she whispered. "He's gone and done it."

"What? What did he do?" Jess asked, her eyes drinking in the sight of Laarn. Like his brother next to him, and the rest of the assembled warriors, he was naked to the waist. She heard the whispers of awe and saw the way the warriors he passed looked at him and the scars covering his body. She knew what they meant, knew they marked his standing as the best healer in the empire, but all she wanted to do was kiss each and every one of them to remove the memory of the pain he must have suffered.

Cat's tone was still shocked. "He's officially named Laarn as Lord Healer. There's no way he can wriggle out of it now."

Unable to tear her gaze away from Laarn as he

stood next to his brother—Hells, why didn't he strip more often? The guy was *ripped*—Jess leaned toward her a little. "Why would he want to wriggle out of it? From what I've heard everyone already considers him lord healer anyway."

"They do," Cat confirmed. "But now he's been named, it would mean he will be based at the healer's hall here on Lathar Prime rather than being able to head off on one of the K'Vass ships whenever he wants."

"Ahhh, I see." Jess settled back in her seat, her gaze still riveted to the big healer in the middle of the arena as he bowed to the emperor and then turned and took a place at the front of the rest of the warriors next to his brother.

And she did. Laarn didn't strike her as the type of man who liked his movements curtailed, so being restricted to a planet probably wouldn't impress him any. At the same time, though, she couldn't help feeling relieved. The Lathar were a warrior culture, as apt to fight amongst themselves for power and position as within the empire, so being on a ship was far more dangerous than being on their home planet. And, from what she'd heard, the healer's hall was considered neutral ground. No one fought there, which meant Laarn would be safe there. Although she knew he was a warrior, the thought of him being in danger made her chest tighten uncomfortably.

As it was now, seeing him on the sands in front of her was okay, she told herself. This was a tournament of skill, not a battle. They weren't seriously trying to kill each other.

"Before we start, warriors may take a moment to claim a token from their females to aid them in battle," Daaynal offered, his arms spread widely to give the warriors on the sands permission to leave it for a moment.

As expected, both Tarrick and Karryl immediately broke formation to walk across the sands toward the pavilion where the human women were sitting, and Jess suddenly realized the purpose of the silken ribbons they'd all been given to wrap around their wrists by the servants upon sitting down.

"My Moore Cat," Tarrick murmured, a smile on his lips as he came to stand in front of his wife. "If you would be so kind?"

Jess smiled as Cat stood, the elevation of the pavilion meaning she stood equal height with her taller husband, and tied the purple ribbon from her wrist around his upper arm. Swooping in for a kiss, he only stopped when he was jostled aside by Karryl even though there was plenty of room for all the women to stand at the front edge of the pavilion.

"Com'on, we don't have all day and you're not the only male here with a mate to impress."

Tarrick chuckled, ceding his place to the big warrior as he beckoned to Jane. The kiss he bestowed on the tall marine was no surprise, but what did make Jess' eyes widen was the fact that two men stood behind Karryl.

She had a brief glimpse of the emperor's champion, Xaandril, whose gaze was locked onto Kenna as he stood in front of them. It was the first time she'd seen the big warrior look anything other than supremely confident as he held out his arm in silence.

But then her breath was taken away as the fourth warrior stepped out from behind Xaandril. Laarn. Two strides brought him to the edge of the pavilion, right in front of her. With a start she found herself standing at the edge of the platform in front of him.

"My lady," Laarn said quietly, meeting her eyes with an unreadable expression. "I would be honored to wear your colors… if you find me worthy to."

She couldn't help it. Her gaze slid down his body, from the long unbound hair across his broad shoulders, over the heavy muscles of his chest and downward toward the cobblestone abs. Heat hit her broadside, swirling through her blood and settling into a hard knot between her thighs. Hell, he was gorgeous... and dressed in just warrior's leathers, hot as fucking hell.

"I do." Her voice breathy, she tried to untie the ribbons at her wrist but fumbled it. The knots tightened and she swore under her breath, trying to get them loose, but the edges of the ribbons had wound themselves around each other like a couple of mating snakes.

"Fuck it," she hissed, trying harder to undo them. "Sorry about this."

"Here." He snagged a hand around her wrist and pulled her closer. "Let me."

His long, strong fingers made short work of the knots. He pulled the ribbon free all too quickly and handed it to her with a small smile.

"Does it matter where I tie it?" she asked, sliding a glance sideways to see Kenna had tied her light blue ribbon around Xaandril's wrist, just above his leather bracer.

Laarn's lip quirked a little at the side. "No. The lady picks the location... as long as I don't have to undress."

She darted a glance up to meet his eyes, finding

warm amusement in the green depths. The heat and arousal in her body hit fever pitch as she imagined peeling the leathers from his body.

"My eyes are up here, beautiful." His soft murmur made her snap her gaze up to meet his again and her cheeks burned in reaction. Shit, she had *so* not been ogling him, right here in front of everyone, had she? The small grin on his face and the chuckle from behind her said that she had. Fucking hell.

"Come here." She stepped in closer and reached up to quickly braid the ribbon through a section of his hair, tying it off in a knot rather than a bow. "There. How's that?"

He inclined his head a little, the dusky pink of her ribbon a bright flash in the dark locks. "You honor me," he said quietly, his fingertips brushing the inside of her wrist. "Later, if I prove myself in battle, I will claim another token. Perhaps one more... physical."

Yes, oh hell yes. She didn't get the chance to reply as he dropped her wrist and turned back toward the sands, dark hair moving like a cape across his broad shoulders as he went.

"Well... wasn't *that* a turn up for the books?" Cat commented, a look of interest in two sets of eyes as she and Jane turned to consider both Kenna and Jess. "Seems you two have been keeping secrets, haven't you?"

"Later," Kenna cut her off, nodding toward the arena. "It's all about to start."

Laarn was on cloud fucking nine.

Not only had Jess given him her token, but she'd looked at him. Actually looked at *him*, at his body. The heat he'd seen in her eyes said she'd seen him as a *man,* not his scars. That look would remain stored in his memory forever and even now, as he faced off against the third warrior in his group, the memory was enough to send a bolt of lust through his body.

He growled as the male in front of him launched an attack so predictable he could have countered it in his sleep. How the male had gotten this far, onto the sands for a tournament, he had no clue, but one thing was for sure. He was leaving the competition right now.

Moving like a *liras* snake, Laarn sidestepped the clumsy attack and reached out as the warrior rushed past him. Two fingers jammed into the side of the male's neck hit the nerve plexus and made the left side of his body less responsive. It wasn't much, barely noticeable as he turned to face off against Laarn again, a snarl on his face. But against Laarn, it would make *all* the difference.

Everything around them—the noise of the crowds, the other fights going on in the other challenge circles, the fact that behind him and to his left Jess watched him—fell away as Laarn's focus narrowed to this moment in time, to just the two of them and the circle of sand they stood in.

Fighting was like surgery. It required utter focus, dedication and skill. In the operating theater, he fought a one-man war against death or permanent injury, both far more fearsome opponents than the male opposite him. He was big-built, almost as big as Karryl or Daaynal, but heavier-set, the slight layer of fat over the carved muscles indicating a fondness for good food and wines.

Laarn didn't smile. Instead, he lifted his hand and beckoned the warrior.

The bull-like warrior snarled and charged again. Laarn waited until he could practically smell the male's breath before he launched his counterattack. Two running steps launched him right at his opponent, the move so quick the other male barely had time to widen his eyes in surprise before Laarn had planted a booted foot on his thigh. Launching himself upward, he arched back, snapping his leading leg out to slam it up and under his opponent's jaw.

There was the sickening crunch of bone and a strangled sound of pain as the other warrior dropped like a stone. Laarn landed lightly on his feet, bringing his guard up immediately, just in case his opponent was still capable of an attack. But the male wasn't... sprawled out on the sand with a stunned expression on his face.

Healers and tournament officials swarmed over to them. Two healers dropped to their knees next to the fallen man, quickly checking him over as one of the officials grabbed Laarn's wrist to raise it and declare him the winner.

"No," he argued, looking over his shoulder to where his opponent was still being seen to. "Brother, are you okay?"

He got a raised fist from the fallen man, just visible from behind the nearest healer, and then... a thumbs up. Laarn bit back a chuckle and made a mental note to check up on the warrior's treatment after the tournament was over.

"And the winner is... Laarn K'Vass!" the official bellowed, holding Laarn's wrist aloft.

The crowd nearby erupted into cheers but Laarn didn't care about them. His gaze cut immediately to the pavilion where Jess sat with the other women. His heart leapt as he saw her rise to her feet, looking at him with a smile on her face as she clapped with the rest of the crowd. Their gazes locked and the smile dropped from her face as she looked at him. Even with the distance between them, awareness stretched taut and Laarn realized the inevitable...

When the tournament was over, she was his. He would claim her as every cell in his body ached to. He knew it, and now she knew it, a flush rising on her cheeks as she dropped her gaze from his. A smile curved the corner of his lips as he waited and, sure enough, a couple of seconds later she snuck another look at him from under her lashes, something he'd noticed she did often. Usually when she thought he wasn't looking in the lab.

Later, he promised himself and turned to see who his next opponent might be. Before the officials could announce it, though, two leather-clad warriors approached the emperor, bots standing guard behind them. At the sight of the combat bots in the palace, Laarn straightened up. That wasn't normal.

One look at the expression on his uncle's face told him it wasn't and the situation was serious.

Daaynal nodded and rose to his feet, holding his hands out for silence.

"My apologies, ladies and gentlemen, but I am afraid I need to pull two fighters from the tournament. Lord Healer Laarn and Xaandril, my champion, would you please attend me?" he asked, indicating they should approach the dais with the throne. Laarn exchanged a look with the big champion as they walked toward the emperor, but the big man's expression indicated he was as in the dark as Laarn was.

"Please... continue with the tournament. Lord K'Vass... you are excused from the tournament to preside in my place, with your delightful lady wife of course."

7

Laarn said nothing as he followed the emperor and his champion into the palace after the messengers. He wasn't surprised at being pulled into such a meeting with the two most powerful men in the empire, not after Daaynal had named him as lord healer in front of everyone at the tournament. Sure, he still had to undergo the lord healer's trial, but that was nothing compared to his healer's trial, a mere formality as he claimed the position. All that mattered was that the emperor had named him, and now his path was set. No getting out of it. Once Daaynal had made his mind up, that was it.

The Emperor made his way into the war-room, turning to watch the rest of them file in. The last to enter were the two messengers, their combat bots taking position to guard the door outside. Laarn frowned. Why were bots being used in place of guards?

"Tell them what you told me," Daaynal ordered the messengers, motioning toward Laarn and Xaandril. The big champion had leaned his hips back against the nearby conference table, arms folded over his broad chest. Laarn took a moment to flick a glance over the guy's markings. Drawn in *serranas* blood and burned right into his skin, they marked all the battles he'd been in over the years. It was an old tradition, not often practiced anymore, not to the extent Xaandril did anyway. Occasionally a warrior marked an important battle. Both he and Tarrick had a starburst marking on their upper arm from their first major battle, but they hadn't bothered since.

The messengers turned, and Laarn easily read the exhaustion on their faces as well as the way the one on the left held himself stiffly, favoring his left side as though he had sustained an injury there. The one on the right, obviously the senior warrior, spoke.

"We've been patrolling the outer borders for the last couple of months," he started and coughed. When his hand came away, Laarn caught the telltale flash of scarlet in his palm. He was right. Both men had been in battle, recently. The messenger continued, "There's been increased activity on the borders. Trade, bounty hunters, general unrest and movement. Several colonies and outposts were attacked and at first we thought it was the Krynassis—"

Xaandril hissed at the mentioned of the reptilian race, but Laarn ignored him. The champion's dislike of reptiles was well known.

"But it wasn't? How do you know?" he asked, a frown between his brows. The reptilian warrior race had always caused issues, nibbling at the edges of the empire's territory or even bold enough to raid colony worlds within it, carrying off whatever supplies and slaves they could get their grubby, clawed hands on.

The warrior shook his head. "We were approached by one of their hive queens, the ruling one in the area. She confirmed that their nests are also being targeted... by Lathar. Fortunately for us, she also knew the identity of the clans involved. Apparently, as the queen closest to our borders, she's been keeping an eye on our politics. She knew these particular clans are not currently in favor."

"Really?" Daaynal had his arms folded across his

chest, rubbing at his stubbled chin with a massive hand. Even though he was undoubtedly male, when he looked like that, a keen light in his green eyes, Laarn saw echoes of his dead mother in her *litaan.* "Interesting. They've never shown such awareness before."

The warrior shrugged. "It seems there's been a massive upheaval in their society. There was an uprising, their Brood Queen was challenged and killed, which has filtered down through the Hive Queens. Most have been replaced with more... forward-thinking females, it seems. Still deadly though. We nearly lost a warrior after he hit on one of her guards."

Laarn lifted an eyebrow. The reptiles had females, he knew that. He had even seen a few and had to admit they were striking in their own way. He'd never wanted to take one to bed, though. He probably wouldn't survive the damn night, no matter how attractive she was. Besides, his tastes ran to curvy little Terrans called Jess these days. A fond smile curved his lips and heat rolled through him at the memory of her look as she'd tied her favor in his hair. She would be his soon. *Very* soon.

"So, which clans?" he asked, bringing the conversation back to the point at hand.

"Three. D'Faran, F'Naar and R'Zaa."

Xaandril and Daaynal exchanged a look.

"No surprise there," the champion grunted. "Those three have been a pain in the ass for years one way or another." He fixed his gaze on the emperor. "Are you finally going to let me go kick their asses to the afterlife and back?"

Daaynal ran a hand through his hair, scooping the loose strands back off his face and snapping a band from his wrist around it.

"I think we have to. If those two have linked up with D'Faran, this isn't just clan leaders being a little pissy... they could field a war group big enough to cause serious damage if they tried to take Lathar Prime."

Laarn rubbed his chin and then suddenly became aware it was an almost identical gesture to the one his uncle had used. Quickly he dropped his hand in case they thought he was imitating the emperor. "They won't attempt to take the home system," he said.

"Think about it. D'Faran have purist tendencies, and both the others got soundly spanked by the Terran women... Kenna held a pistol to J'aett's head in front of all his men in the main courtyard and Jane blew Ishaan F'Naar's brains out on his own ship for poisoning Karryl. No, they won't come for Lathar Prime... they'll go for Earth itself. Remove the problem at the source."

"Shit," Xaandril breathed. "He's right. They will."

"Not happening." Daaynal's voice was firm as he straightened up. "Not on my watch. Xaan, you take a war group and head out to the borders. Stop the bastards before they can mobilize. Stop them at any cost. Laarn, take a team of combat healers and go with him. I suspect your expertise will be needed—both on the battlefield and in the healer's bay."

"Yes, sire," both men replied automatically, knowing not to argue when the emperor used that tone of voice, and turned to follow the messengers out.

"Laarn, a moment, please."

He turned at the order, waiting as the others filed out. He tilted his head as he looked over at his uncle. "Your Majesty?"

Daaynal waved in irritation. "Cut the crap when it's just us. Daaynal will do just fine." His gaze was firm. "Make sure you see your little human before you go and cement your claim. I do not want to have to fight fires over females while you're gone, understand me? Especially not one so important to us."

Laarn inclined his head, hiding his determined expression. "Don't worry. Before I go she'll know she belongs to me."

"You're leaving? Now?"

Worried, Jess had slipped away while the tournament was still ongoing to find Laarn in his lab again. This time, though, he wasn't working. Instead, he was packing cases with medical equipment.

"Yes," he replied, his expression grim and his long hair dancing over his broad shoulders. He didn't look at her at first, carefully packing some medical gadget into a padded case and then adding it to a bigger one. "The situation on the outer borders has gone into meltdown. The emperor has ordered a war group to head out and check the situation. Apparently, some colonies have been destroyed, so healers will be required."

"Destroyed?" Her eyes widened. "Will you be safe?"

Worry coiled in her gut, her heart clenching at the thought of him in danger. A chuckle rumbling in the back of his throat, he appeared in front of her suddenly. Sliding a big hand into her hair, he used his thumb under her chin to make her look up and meet his eyes.

"Did you not just see me out on the sands, little one?" he asked, his eyes and voice warm. A shiver hit her as he crushed her cheek with his thumb in a soft caress. "I might be a healer, but I'm Lathar... I'm a warrior born and bred. I'll heal, but I can also kill without mercy. Especially to save my people... and the ones I love."

His voice dropped on the last words, his gaze latching onto her lips. Before she knew it, he'd crowded her back against the counter behind her, his big body cutting off her view of the rest of the room. The air between them heated as he looked down at her, intent written over his face as he slowly bent, lowering his lips to hers.

She moaned, bringing her hands up to his broad chest. This time, instead of the jacket he usually wore, she got to touch his skin. Like the rest of him, it was warm and hard, silky to the touch. The kiss was softer than any he'd given her before. He teased her lips, feathering his mouth over hers as though he were learning the shape and texture of them before he nibbled lightly on her lower lip. She parted them with a whimper, needing more of him, his kisses, but he didn't take her up on the offer.

Instead, he carried on with the soft nips, his free hand sliding around her waist to pull her up firmly against him.

She registered the thick, full hardness of his cock pressed against her softer belly and gasped. He was huge, she'd known that, but to feel it pressed against her again took her breath away... and sent thick, dark heat swirling through her body. Anticipation and need weakened her limbs as she clung to him, pressing herself to him in invitation and hoping he'd deepen the kiss, claim her lips like he had before.

He chuckled again at her eagerness, and this time, gave in to her silent demands. Releasing her lip from his teeth, the pressure of his fingers at the back of her neck tilted her lips up for him and he claimed them. She whimpered as he invaded her mouth, sliding his tongue against hers and back again in an erotic dance that fired every cell in her body. Where he'd learned to kiss like that, like a sex god, when the Lathar had no women, she didn't know. It didn't matter. All that did was that he was here, with her.

The kiss started off soft and sweet, slow and languorous, but within seconds, any sweetness disappeared. Heat built and exploded as his kiss grew harder and hotter. A growl in the back of his throat, he pulled her tighter into his body, his hands on her just this side of cruel. But she didn't care, the same feral need gripped her as she slid her hands over his shoulders and chest, the satin of his skin highlighted by the smooth scars as she touched him.

With a gasp he broke away, leaning his forehead against hers. His chest heaved as he fought for breath, and, she realized, control.

"Not here," he said in a voice just this side of a growl. "Not now. I need to go..." At her small cry of protest, the corners of his lips quirked. "When I take you, little one, it won't be a quick fuck snatched before I have to leave. It'll be all night, all day... and everyone in the palace will hear my name on your lips as you scream."

She shivered, biting her lip as she looked up at him.

"Don't look at me that way..." He swore, the heavy Latharian words almost unintelligible. His features just this side of feral, he claimed her lips again in a hard kiss before breaking away. "Perhaps something to remember me by..."

Before she realized what he was doing, he'd boosted her up onto the counter, shoving his hips between her parted thighs to drink from her lips again. She whimpered, the soft sound one of submission as she opened up for him. The answering male growl did things to her on a primal level, and a second later she felt his hand on her leg under her skirts as it slid upward. Her breathing caught as he reached her thigh, and she parted wider for him, arching her back. His rumble of approval was lost under their kiss as he thrust his tongue into her mouth again to seek hers.

His questing fingers reached the juncture of her thighs and a thread of amusement rolled through her as he started, realizing that she didn't wear any underwear. Breaking away from their kiss, he looked down at her, the light color of his eyes swallowed up by darkness. "Only ever leave your underthings off for me," he demanded. "No other male… not unless you want him dead."

Unable to speak, she just nodded, her breathing catching when he swept blunt-tipped fingers between her folds. They were slick, wet with the evidence of her arousal, which he gathered, smoothing the slickness up and over her clit. "This is mine, little Jess," he murmured, lips against her jaw and the side of her throat. "I'll have your release before I go, my name on your lips, but when I get back… you're mine. Understand?"

She nodded, breathless with anticipation as his fingers explored her pussy lips, grazing against her swollen clit. Her breath caught at the slight contact and she arched her back, rocking her hips to try and get more sensation. He chuckled, hot mouth on her skin, and nipped her earlobe.

"Eager for me, are you, little one?" he murmured, the tip of his broad finger circling her pussy. She whimpered as he breached her body just a little before withdrawing.

"Not yet, I don't think..." he breathed, kissing a trail of fire down her neck. Every cell in her body was focused on the path of his lips and that of his fingers as they stroked through her swollen pussy lips, slick with her own desire. He found her clit again, and she stiffened for a second. Then she whimpered as pleasure rolled through her, exploding out from her clit to fill her blood.

He murmured soft words in his own language as he kissed her and circled her clit in small strokes. Lifting her hands, she clung to his broad shoulders, her fingers biting in as he drove her nearly insane with his touch. Her clit ached with each stroke and she arched toward him, offering him more of herself. She needed more, needed his touch... needed *him*.

He moved, sliding a thick finger deep inside her. She whimpered, pressing her forehead to his shoulder as he slid it back and in again. Adding a second finger, he used his free hand to tilt her head back.

"No, Jess, I want to see you. I want to see what I do to you. I want to see the expression on your face when I make you come. Your pleasure, the pleasure I give to you, is *mine*. Understand?"

She swallowed, nodding and biting her lip as he added another finger to slide deep. Her needy pussy clenched, gripping him as he fucked her with the long digits, pressing his thumb to her aching clit. His gaze locked to hers, she couldn't look away. Her breath came in short pants and then a groan as he turned his hand and curled his fingers back to press against her g-spot.

"So sensitive," he murmured, his expression tense and focused on her. "So tight... I'm going to enjoy making you mine. Stretching this sweet little pussy around my thick cock. Will you like that, little Jess... being taken and fucked by a warrior?"

Unable to speak, she nodded, a whimper falling from her lips as her hips began to move, rocking with his motions as her body tightened. Ripples of sensation fluttered through her, centering in her pussy. They grew stronger and tighter, her movements more needy until she was riding his hand, desperate to come.

"Laarn..." she begged. "Please. I need..."

His expression hardened, his eyes laser-focused on hers. "Come," he ordered. "Now."

It was as if her body had been waiting for his words, and rapture exploded through her, spiraling out from her core as she came around his fingers in a hot rush. The force of it sapped her strength, forcing her to cling to him more as she rode out the waves. He held her against his broad chest, stroking her through it. His thumb on her clit drew out the sensations until she shivered, lying limply against his chest and shoulder.

"You look wonderful when you come," he murmured by her ear, "a sight I fully intend to enjoy again, soon, as you come all over my cock when I take you as mine."

Pulling his hand from her, he lifted it to his lips and licked her essence from his fingers. The groan was purely masculine and full of hunger, a hunger that blazed in his eyes as he looked down at her.

"You're mine, Jess. Remember that because I'll be back."

8

Laarn had been gone for nearly a week. Days without word from the battle group. Jess found herself jumping each time a door swished open, in case it was one of the emperor's men to update them on the situation.

But it wasn't. Apart from a simple message from Daaynal that all was proceeding as normal, they'd received no word from the battlefront.

"This is ridiculous! They must know something!" Kenna exploded into movement, leaping up from the low couches they'd been reclining on in the garden room attached to their suite. A pleasant breeze swept in from outside, but neither woman noticed the lovely summer day outside. Instead, Kenna was too busy pacing, a pissed expression on her face, and Jess herself was too... empty to enjoy the weather.

Instead, all she could think of was Laarn and the way he'd kissed her before he left. His clever fingers under her skirts, sliding into her pussy and against her clit to bring her to the strongest climax she'd ever had in her life. Everything seemed dull and flat without him here.

"I'm sure they'd have told us," she said flatly, not watching as Kenna paced the exquisitely tiled floor. There was just the two of them in the suite, both Cat and Jane having gone with their husbands to the front.

"They should have," the marine growled. "There's no way they're stupid enough as a warrior race to lose communications, so they *have* to be in contact with Xaan and his ships."

Jess looked up, mustering a small smile despite her misery. "Oh... Xaan, is it?" she teased lightly. "Should we expect wedding bells soon?"

"Bite me, Kallson," Kenna snarled back, flipping her the bird. "We're just friends."

At that Jess did chuckle. "That old chestnut? Spin me another."

"You can talk," Kenna shot back. "Mooning about after the healer... fuck, we're as bad as each other." She paused in front of the door, indecision on her face. "Fuck it. I'm going to get some answers. Daaynal *will* talk to me, even if I have to fucking sleep outside his door. You coming?" she asked, arching an eyebrow in question.

Jess shook her head. "No, I feel a little odd," she said, pressing her hand over her stomach. "I think I'm going to head down to the medbay and get checked out. I think something I ate yesterday disagreed with me."

"Okay, love. I'll come find you if I get answers. Send someone for me if you need me, okay?"

Jess nodded, but the other woman was already gone before she'd finished hauling herself off the low couch. Her movements sluggish, she headed out of the women's suite and made her way toward the medbay.

Once she got there though, she couldn't face the thought of explaining to any of the healers, all tall, imposing Lathar with serious expressions who always seemed to look down their noses at her. They seemed to dislike her intently, possibly because she was here so often for tests. Why they didn't like her for that, though, she didn't know. Surely all efforts toward solving the problem were a good thing, right?

Obviously not. As soon as the doors swished

open, they all studiously ignored her, obviously finding their screens more interesting than helping her. She shrugged to herself and walked through the main lab, heading for Laarn's personal lab at the back. With the ridiculously advanced level of their technology, she was fairly sure she didn't need them to find out if she had a stomach bug or not anyway. All she needed was to boot up one of those fancy diagnostic beds and have the computers scan her. She'd seen Laarn do it so many times, she was sure she could figure it out herself.

As she approached the back of the room, heading toward the double doors that led to Laarn's lab, she resisted the urge to bite her lip in worry. She was going to look a right idiot if, with Laarn away, the lab didn't let her in. But before she was within ten feet of the doors, the lights within flickered on and the doors swished open in front of her. Breathing a sigh of relief, she walked in and just stood in the center of the space for a moment as the doors shut behind her.

It was strange being in here without him, but there were reminders of him everywhere she looked. One of his sashes, teal to mark his role as a healer, hung on a hook on the wall next to a warrior's leather jacket. On the counter to her left, the one he'd boosted her on and brought her to the most earth-shattering climax, was his mug. She couldn't read Latharian, but she was fairly sure it was a humorous one, something along the lines of "Trust me, I'm a doctor."

To her right was his office area, the surface of the desk littered with not paper, but the thin sheets of plastic-like material the Lathar used, all with Laarn's distinctive scrawl across them. She could even smell his scent in the air, a combination of warm, clean man and some kind of citrus. That was one thing she'd noticed from the moment she'd met him... he smelled *so* good.

Closing her eyes for a moment, she drew a deep breath into her lungs and imagined he was here. It eased some of the ache in the center of her chest.

Opening her eyes, she brought herself back to reality and focused on the matter at hand. "I don't feel well," she announced to the air around her, knowing the lab's AI system would be listening.

It was. The diagnostic bed in the middle of the floor lit up, the flashing lights running down the side of the padded mattress a silent invitation to lie down. Crossing the floor on slippered feet, Jess boosted herself up backward and swung her legs up to lie down in the middle. Once she had, the holo-arch lit up and she watched as the lights whirled and raced over it, scanning her.

"Subject scan complete. Patient alpha five seven nine, Jessica Kallson. Human female," the AI announced. *"Several in-progress tests for this subject. One complete and viable. Proceed?"*

She nodded. Laarn always did a lot of tests on her to make sure she was fit and healthy before he moved on to analyzing her DNA. It seemed the bed was still set up in that routine. "Yes, please."

"Compliance."

The lights whirled again, centering on her abdomen. She watched as they got faster and faster, and then the bed hummed like it was about to take off. Heat washed over her stomach for a moment, starting low down, just over her pelvis, and then washing up. A gasp broke from her lips at the intensity, but within a heartbeat it was gone as though it had never been there. Her hands went instantly to her stomach, expecting to find the fabric of her gown hot, but it wasn't. The silk was just skin-warmed from the heat of her body within, nothing more. Huh, odd.

"Computer? Is that it? Am I okay?" she ventured as the holo-arch clicked off.

"Affirmative. Subject is running a slight temperature

and scan reports slight gastro-intestinal distress but no viral or bacterial cause found. Recommend rest and light repast until condition resolves."

She was okay. Jess breathed a sigh of relief. She'd been right, it must have been something she ate.

"Thank you, computer. Can I go now?" she asked as politely as if she'd been speaking to a flesh and blood medic. Since Laarn had told her the lab computer was a sentient AI, she'd treated it as a person, albeit an invisible one. It was only right.

"Affirmative. Please return at the same time tomorrow for condition check."

"Err..." Jess paused in the middle of sliding off the bed. "Sure, if you need me to."

The computer didn't reply, but the lights at the back of the lab started to shut down. Obviously the AI was done with her. With a small shrug, Jess headed out of the lab, ignoring the healers in the main medbay as she left.

"Move on the left flank!"
"Hold your fire! Wait for it...NOW!"
"Retreat! Retreat!"
"Don't let the bastards get away!"

Laarn kept his head down as he made his way through the battlefield, his team around him. Two *drakeen* battle bots fought not a hundred feet away, arm cannons moving continuously as they swept the area for enemy forces that might have lingered after the battle.

The big healer watched for a moment, noting the idiosyncrasies of the bots' movements. There weren't many *drakeen*-capable pilots in the battle group. From the way the one on the left moved, Kraan was piloting, which meant the other one was Isan. The other pilots would be off duty, sleeping, apart from Jathor, who had been killed in action yesterday.

Laarn's heart ached for a moment. Jath had been in his and Tarrick's training group during their childhood, a quick and capable warrior with a sharp sense of humor who had dreamed of finding his bond-mate. He'd been so excited at the news of the human women, sure his mate would be amongst them. He'd never gotten to meet them all and find out, bleeding out on a battlefield in the arse-end of beyond fighting traitors.

Laarn turned, his split second of reflection over. Combat bots raced to fill the gaps between the combat teams and the bigger *drakeen*. His medical pack over his back and a rifle in his hand, he kept an eye out as his team moved behind him.

Even now, without battle raging around them, they operated like a combat unit, moving further into the battlefield as they checked for wounded. Some were beyond help, their bodies simply tagged with locator beacons as the team moved on... others were more fortunate, able to be treated and walk out themselves. The badly injured were locator-tagged and evac'ed by bots as soon as they could be.

But that wasn't why Laarn was here. Normally in a battle situation, he was far behind the lines, fighting a war of his own in surgery as he battled death and serious injury to bring a warrior from the brink. But not today.

"*Anyone sees the general,*" he bellowed. "*I want to know. Immediately.*"

His team nodded, a chorus of affirmative responses through his earpiece as they spread out to check the ground the battle had swept through. The word had come through early this morning about an attack through the southern lines, which they hadn't been expecting. Xaandril had taken a company to check it out.

Hours later, three men had returned, battered and bloody, to say it had been a trick. Some of the men within the company had been traitors, purist sympathizers, and the battle had turned into a bloodbath. The general had been lost, last seen fighting ten men and a bot as he held a break in the lines all by himself. Then enemy reinforcements had arrived... No one had seen him fall, but he must have. No warrior could face such odds and win.

The senior warrior, Laarn had been forced to assume command of the entire war group, his duties as healer taking a back seat as he gave orders and sent men into battle. He had gone into battle himself, a rifle in his hand and any mercy he had from his healer's calling locked down tight. It had been brutal and bloody, but eventually they had emerged the victors, sending the traitorous combined forces fleeing broken for their lives. Now, they were on cleanup and body recovery detail.

"Come on, Xaandril," Laarn muttered to himself, scanning bodies as he walked.

"Drag the enemy to the edge of the battlefield," he ordered. "We'll set a pyre before we go to make sure the predators don't get to them."

"More than they deserve," Kriis, the warrior walking next to him, muttered. "Should leave them to get their eyes pecked out and eaten."

"Yeah," Laarn sighed. "I know. But that makes us

no better than them and besides, this many bodies? It'll stink the place up for the locals and foul their water supply. They might be no better than oonat, but they didn't ask for this war, or what those assholes did to them. We have a responsibility to try and put things right, or at the least, not leave them fucked up."

"Yeah, I see what you mean," Kriis replied, but his expression was distracted. "Errr... Lord Healer, over here." He broke into a run, sliding to his knees to shove a dead R'Zaa warrior to the side, revealing a male covered in blood. Laarn's heart lurched as he recognized the pale, cropped hair.

The general.

His knees hit the dirt next to Xaandril a heartbeat after Kriis', his experienced gaze sweeping the big warrior.

"Okay, we got multiple injuries... that arm is badly broken. Looks like a gut wound. Get some pressure on that," he ordered, sticking his fingers into the guy's throat. It was too slick with blood and mangled flesh for him to feel anything, so Laarn switched to his wrist and sighed with relief. Xaandril's pulse flickered, weak but there.

"Okay, he's still with us. Get some bots in here," he ordered, snapping out a handheld diagnostic unit and sweeping it over the form of his fallen friend. It bleeped, churning out a list of near devastating injuries.

"*Draanth,* my friend," Laarn breathed. "How you're not dead, I do not know."

Putting the diag-unit down by his thigh, he reached into his pack and snapped together some pressure-sprays, using combination medications that would hopefully hold the general's condition as it was until Laarn could get him into surgery. Pulling the wounded man's bracer away from his wrist, Laarn paused as he spotted the flash of a light blue ribbon. For a moment he smiled, flicking a glance up at the big man's face to find Xaandril watching him, his eyes dark with pain.

"Don't worry, my friend, I'll get you back to her," Laarn promised and pressed the spray to Xaandril's wrist. He nodded a little and his eyes closed as the medication took effect.

Laarn stood up as the bots arrived. He carefully lifted the fallen warrior onto a stretcher and turned to the warrior next to him. Before he could speak though, laser fire sliced through the air.

"*Take cover!*" Laarn bellowed, his rifle off his back in an instant as he took a position in front of the bots loading Xaandril onto the stretcher. His keen gaze easily picked out the aggressors, hidden in a small copse nearby. Just warriors, not bots with them. "In the trees!" he shouted as the warriors with him all took cover and started firing back. The *drakeen* tank-bots lumbered into place, hunkering down on their six crab-like legs and using their bulk to protect the healers and their patient.

"Lord Healer!" One of the healers shouted, waving for him to take cover behind the safety of the bot wall but Laarn shook his head. These assholes had picked the wrong fight.

"Moving!" he shouted, not waiting for a confirmation as he broke cover and ran toward the trees. Laser bolts peppered the air around him, keeping the enemy's head down as he dashed for cover again. His heart thrilled with the joy of battle as he crashed through the tree line, three warriors on his heels. A war cry broke from his lips as he slung the rifle on its strap over his back again and pulled the big blade from the sheath across his shoulders.

The enemy—R'Zaa warriors he realized as soon as he got a look at their faces—were on them in a hot-second. Half their number broke away from the firefight and raced toward Laarn and his group with blades drawn. He bared his teeth as battle was joined, his blade clashing against that of the first warrior to reach them. Blocking the blow, Laarn let the male's blades slide down his to the guard and twisted, trapping his opponent's blade. As he did, he lifted his free arm and slammed his elbow up and into the guy's jaw.

Bone crunched under the blow, and the male staggered back, his blade falling from his hand as he grabbed for his shattered jaw. Lifting his blade, Laarn swung with brutal force, taking the R'Zaa's head off at the shoulders. It bounced away, and he stepped over the falling body to meet the next warrior.

His blade rose and fell as he sliced and parried, cutting a swathe through the enemy. The fight was bloody and brutal, but within minutes he stood, blood dripping from his blade and the bodies of his enemies lying at his feet. His chest heaved as he sucked in air, and he was covered in blood as he turned around and found the small team that had followed him looking at him with a mix of awe and something near fear.

"Never make an enemy of a man who can dissect you in his sleep," he commented in a low voice, leaning down to wipe his bloody blade on one of the men he'd killed.

"Pick up the rest of the wounded and survivors," he ordered as he emerged from the copse and approached the rest of his men. Turning, he strode after the bots carrying Xaandril toward the waiting shuttle. "And get everyone off the planet's surface before the predators come out at nightfall."

"Yes, my lord. Of course." One of the younger warriors peeled away, setting about his task without argument. Laarn didn't spare him a glance, his boots ringing out on the metal ramp as he boarded. Watching the bots lock Xaandril's bio-stretcher down, he patched his comms into the war group through the shuttle's array and opened a channel.

"This is the lord healer. I have the general. He's badly injured but alive. Prep the main surgery bay for our arrival and have healer teams standing by for my orders."

9

Even though she'd been checked out and the medical AI had said her condition would ease, a few days later Jess was feeling no better. In fact, she was feeling decidedly worse. The feelings of stomach discomfort had increased to actual nausea and she felt hot all over, the kind of clammy hot all over that didn't bode well.

Groaning, she turned on her side and looked toward the door of her bedroom. She'd returned to lie down after lunch, but the nap hadn't done her any good. Instead, now she was seriously worried. Something was wrong. Very, very wrong. She needed to go to the medbay.

Her entire body ached as she pulled herself to the edge of the bed. The effort made her light-headed, shivers running over her skin as she made her way to the door. The room spun around her, the walls moving as she made her way through the main room of the women's quarters and into the corridor beyond.

"Lady Jessica! I was hoping to see you," a familiar deep voice sounded behind her.

Spinning on her heel, Jess overshot and stumbled... right into Saal's arms. His eyes widened in surprise and for a second heat flared in his eyes.

"I've wanted to get you in my arms for weeks," he murmured, his voice husky and seductive, but almost instantly he frowned. Lifting a hand, he pressed it to her forehead. "Gods, Jessica... you're burning up."

"Medbay," she pleaded, her fingers curled in the edges of his jacket. "I don't feel well. Please, Saal."

"For you, my love, anything."

She didn't argue over his endearment as he swept her up in his arms, too busy trying not to be sick, and she closed her eyes as he carried her through the corridors. His frame was big, warm and reassuring and she relaxed, knowing that she was safe with him. For the moment anyway. Even though he'd eased off trying to claim her since he'd rescued her from the purist guard, she was under no illusions that he had forgotten about it. It was only a matter of time before he tried his luck again. She couldn't think of that at the moment, though, not when her skin felt like it was burning off and her lunch was likely to make another appearance.

"Almost there," he said in a low voice, his breathing not even labored as he hurried through the palace with long strides. "Open up," he ordered, his voice pitched to carry. "Lady Jessica needs a healer. *Now!*"

She heard rather than saw the bustle of medbay around them, still clinging to Saal to stop the awful spinning in her head. He murmured soothingly as he bent to lay her down on a soft surface. Risking a small peek, she found she was in the main bay, healers bustling around them and a steely-faced Daaynal watching them both. She didn't miss the icy expression in his eyes. Shit, he was Laarn's uncle as well. If he thought she was cheating on his nephew... she'd be pissed as well if she were him.

"I felt ill," she explained as the diagnostic bed started up, the arch forming over her in a swirl of interlacing beams. "He found me in the corridor and brought me here."

Daaynal nodded, transferring his attention to the

healers clustered around her. "What's wrong with her? Find out. *Now!*"

Jess relaxed back against the padded mattress with a sigh. Whatever it was, the computers would figure it out, and hopefully give her something. She shuddered violently as a wave of heat, and then cold washed over her, not listening to the voices and bleeps and beeps of the machine anymore. It all merged into one as she slipped into semi-consciousness.

"She's *pregnant?*" Daaynal's stunned voice brought her out of her doze to find the big emperor staring at the healers. Then he turned an accusing glare on Saal. The warrior looked surprised for a moment, and she caught the flash of fury in his eyes before he blinked and covered it, adding a quick, fake smile.

"I'm what?" she asked, but her stomach rebelled and she rolled to her side and puked into the bucket one of the healers held out quickly for her.

"We are blessed," she heard Saal saying, as he patted her calf. *"We weren't sure but had hoped..."*

Nonononono. She tried to shake her head as savage heaves racked her frame, her body purging itself of everything she'd eaten in the last couple of hours, but she couldn't do anything until she'd finished throwing up. A healer gave her a damp cloth and helped her rinse her mouth out before she collapsed weakly back on the bed, her head and shoulders now raised comfortably, to find Saal and Daaynal locked in a battle of wills, steely expressions on both men's faces.

"I claim the Terran, Lady Jessica..." Saal was saying through gritted teeth. "She's carrying my child, so she belongs to me."

Carrying his child... she was pregnant.

"I can't be," she said, her words dropping like a ton weight into the charged silence of the room. "I've never slept with him, nor has he claimed me. I mean, he's *tried,* but—"

"I'm claiming her now," the big warrior insisted. "And I have bedded her. How else is she with child?"

"Lady Jessica?" Daaynal turned toward her, his eyebrow raised. The frosty expression was still on his face but had thawed a little. He wanted to believe her... that much was evident.

She shook her head. "I don't know. I haven't had sex with anyone since I left Earth months ago..."

"Lies!" Saal exclaimed, only to be cut off as the double doors to the medbay swept open.

"He's the one lying," Kenna announced as she swept into the room. "She's been avoiding him because she's worried he'll claim her and she wants Laarn to."

"*Kenna!*" Jess hissed, panic rising along with the bile in her stomach. Quickly she grabbed the fresh bucket a healer held out for her.

"Oh, shut it," the marine ordered in a no-nonsense voice. "You want to be tied to a man you don't want? I got this."

She turned her attention to the two men in the center of the room, her hand not resting on the grip of the pistol at her hip but relaxed beside it. The kind of relaxed that said she could have the thing in hand and firing within a heartbeat. "No one is claiming anyone today. My girl Mary here just got the shock of a lifetime, so let's all back the fuck down and sort out what the hell is going on, shall we?"

Daaynal frowned. "Mary? I thought her name was Jessica."

"It is. It comes from—" Kenna shook her head, her expression bringing an exhausted smile to Jess' lips. "Never mind. It doesn't matter. Jess, how are you feeling?"

"Like I just got out of high-g training after a three-day bender on Tarinat-four," she grumbled, naming one of the rough and ready outpost stations in the Sol Sector. She transferred her attention to

Daaynal. "I have not slept with Saal," she declared firmly. "And I am definitely *not* pregnant by him. I shouldn't be pregnant at all. Are you sure?" she demanded of the healer hovering by her.

He nodded, pulling up a display in front of him and tapping through data she couldn't read until he found the one he wanted. Turning it, he showed her the screen. "See these levels here and here? The scans all indicate a viable pregnancy in the very early stages. I would say no more than two weeks."

"You can tell that early?" She blinked in surprise, looking up at him. While she'd seen him in the main medbay a lot, she didn't recognize what clan he was from. Definitely not a K'Vass that was for sure. He had high cheekbones and an almost exotic look that she'd never seen before.

"Of course," he replied. "Our technology is far more advanced than yours. We can tell from the moment of conception. Even check the child's DNA and extrapolate what it will look like."

Oh my. She just looked at him, unable to take it all in. "So I really *am* pregnant? Can you..." Shit, this was going to sound so bad. "Can you tell who the father is?"

The healer blinked. "You don't know?"

"*Everyone OUT!*" Daaynal ordered, his loud,

commanding growl causing healers and warriors alike to scatter, heading for the double doors at the front of the room. "Even you, Saal. *Now!*"

The big warrior grumbled, looking toward Jess, but she ignored him. Her attention was fixed on the healer, who suddenly looked very nervous. Flicking a glance between the two women, and the emperor, he cleared his throat. While Laarn was away, he was obviously the lead healer, as his scars attested to. They weren't as numerous or as vicious as Laarn's, but certainly more plentiful than the other healers she'd seen in here.

"No," she repeated. "Since I've not slept with a man since I left Earth, I don't know who the father is."

Her hands crept down to cover her stomach in wonder as she spoke. Could it be true? Was she really pregnant, and... how?

The healer frowned. "What does sleeping have to do with procreation?"

Daaynal rumbled in the back of his throat, half a growl and half clearing it. "It's a Terran phrase. It means she hasn't had sex with a male."

"But..." Surprise flowed over his face. "She must have, more than that, she must have had sex with a Lathar warrior..."

"Oh?" Daaynal's gaze sharpened as Jess spluttered. "I can assure you I have *not!*"

"Well, she must have. I can see the human genetic information, but the father was definitely Lathar—"

"Who? What family?" Daaynal demanded, his expression sharp. Jess thought the healer would have a heart attack on the spot, the tension in his frame was so complete as he studied the readings on the screen.

"He took some of my eggs for a test," she said quietly. "He must have fertilized them and implanted them without telling me." It was the only explanation that made sense. Her heart broke as she met the emperor's gaze.

"The baby is Laarn's."

THE SHUTTLE RIDE to the *Keran'vuis,* Xaandril's flagship, was less than ten minutes but seemed like hours as Laarn hovered by the stretcher holding the still form of the general. The big warrior was pale, his wounds standing out stark red against his skin. He wasn't that much older than Laarn, but with his scars and the terrible wounds across his body... he seemed eons older.

"Coming into dock now, my lord," one of the pilots leaned out from the cockpit to inform him.

Laarn nodded, feeling the shuttle slow and the slight bump as the docking clamps engaged. The stasis unit was holding Xaandril's condition steady, but he couldn't remain in it forever. Despite the fact it held death at bay, just, the longer he remained in it, the harder it would be for Laarn to bring him back.

The airlock cycled with heavy whirrs and clunks. Then the door behind him slid open. Laarn was ready, pushing the stretcher out first, scattering the warriors waiting on the other side.

"Move!" he barked in a hard voice, looking through the morass of warriors until he found scars under open jackets and teal sashes. "Is the surgical bay prepared?"

"Yes, my lord... and a support team on standby with a backup healer." A healer shoved his way through the group until he reached Laarn's side, taking over pushing the stretcher as they strode through the corridors.

"We won't need them. This is beyond everything they have," he said, rolling his shoulders as they walked. He needed to be loose and limber for the operation ahead.

Warriors in red sashes trailed behind them, obviously waiting for permission to speak. Their expressions said they plainly didn't like the idea of a healer being in charge but none of them had stepped up to challenge him. He didn't expect them to. Unlike what he'd heard of human medics, who swore to do no harm, healers among the Lathar were something different entirely. They were warriors always and fought if they needed to. Some of the most dangerous warriors in Lathar history had also been healers, his own grandfather among them.

"Orders, my lord?" one of them ventured just before they turned into medbay. Laarn cut him a glance, noting it was one of the general's commanders. Xaandril didn't have a second in command as such, but a team of them. Laarn could see the reasoning. Rather than one person who could directly challenge him for his rank and position, there was a group who had to fight among themselves before they could challenge him. The infighting kept the balance until one emerged strong enough to be named second officer properly.

"Yaraan, right?" Laarn asked, pulling the male's name from his memories of coming aboard nearly a week ago. "Split the war group and create a cordon between this part of space and all routes to Lathar Prime," he ordered. "Keep the patrols tight and capture any of the enemy if you can for interrogation. I want to know what these bastards thought they'd achieve by all this. These colony-worlds hold little value, so it doesn't make sense. Establish contact with the local Krynassis queen. See if you can broker a short-term treaty to deal with this threat, but give no assets away. Understood?"

Through it all, Yaraan stood, his face determined as he nodded. The fact that Laarn spoke directly to him, rather than the other command officers around him meant this was his responsibility.

"Yes, my lord. Loud and clear." He grinned suddenly. "I won't let you down."

"You'd better not." Laarn transferred his attention to the group around Yaraan. "Who commands the general's flagship?"

"That would be me." An older male stepped forward, his manner and bearing screaming experience. "Draxx. Commander of the *Keran'vuis.*"

Laarn nodded to him, conferring the correct respect to the older warrior. To command a flagship was an honor, even more so when it was a general's ship. The only honor higher was commanding the emperor's ship, the *Misaan'vuis,* itself. "Bring us about and set a course for Lathar Prime. The general is in critical condition and I may need the facilities in the healer's hall at the palace to..." he didn't finish his sentence. They all knew the general was in bad shape.

"Aye, sir," the commander nodded and then growled at the warriors clustered around. "Ye heard the lord. Hop to it!"

The warriors scattered, boots thudding on the deck-plating as the corridor cleared. Draxx turned to Laarn, his expression direct. "Save my brother, healer, and I will forever be in your debt."

Laarn blinked in surprise as the big commander turned and walked away. He and Xaandril were brothers? Now he looked at it, he could kind of see the resemblance—in their builds and the way they walked—and it explained why an obviously capable warrior was content to serve under another.

Turning, he walked into the medical bay, putting everything else from his mind as he entered the cleansing unit to prepare for surgery.

10

Xaandril was a mess.

Laarn whistled to himself, looking down at the still form of his patient on the table in front of him. There was a big knife wound across his throat, his left arm was at the wrong angle and the shoulder looked mangled, the ends of his collarbone were visible in what looked like raw meat... his gaze moved down as his assistants moved around him, prepping the surgical unit... two gut wounds and one across the thigh.

"My lord?"

At the prompt, Laarn held his arms out to the side, letting his assistants slide the gauntlets over his hands and tighten the straps over his wrists. They were like a normal pair of gloves to the wrist, but beyond neural cables sprouted like spines, falling to the floor to snake around the operating table with its protective bubble enclosing the patient.

The patient. That's who Xaandril had become now. Laarn was an experienced healer. He knew he couldn't let emotion or friendship enter into him as he prepared to be uplinked.

"Neural interface ready, surgical unit online," his assistant murmured by his side, a shadowy form in the darkness around the brightly lit bed. "Ready when you are, my lord."

Laarn took a deep breath, the scent of disinfectant and under it, blood, hitting his sensitive nose and nodded. "Link me."

The healer reached out and initiated the link, the wires connecting him to the unit flaring to life. He had a moment to gather himself as he felt the first flutter of sensation along the link. His consciousness expanded, flowing from his body to fill the operating unit. It was a similar interface as the one used for the combat and other avatar-bots, allowing him to control the machine through the link, but there were differences.

First, it wasn't a bot. It was far more complicated and sophisticated, requiring much more of his mental processing power and concentration, and secondly, unlike a bot, the link went *both* ways. He and the patient were connected, so whatever he felt, the patient felt... and whatever his patient felt, so did he. Everything...from the way his leathers itched a little where some blood had dried and stiffened them, right through to the pain his patients were in as he operated.

And that was what it meant to be a healer. He not only had to operate and heal them, put broken bodies back together again, but through the neural links, he shouldered their pain during the procedure as well, *felt* the operation from both sides. And that feeling, as well as the highest pain tolerance ever recorded in the healer's trials, was what made Laarn so good at what he did.

"Bringing the patient online."

Another nod.

He closed his eyes as the link expanded, bracing himself. Between one second and the next, pain exploded through him. The grunt that echoed in his chest was all the sound he'd allow himself to make, even though his entire body screamed with agony. Leaning back against the support in the small of his back, he took a deep breath and focused.

"Patient vitals leveling..." His senior assistant kept up a quiet running commentary in the background. Laarn may have nodded in reply, but he wasn't aware of it. Instead, he went within his own mind, following the link down into Xaandril's body. Using the link and the remote surgical arms of the bed, he focused on the most grievous wounds.

Nano-scalpels and regenerators moved faster than the eye could see as he repaired and rebuilt muscle and blood vessels within Xaandril's throat. Meticulously, he built layer upon layer and at the same time kept Xaan's circulatory system moving, making sure not to flood the area with blood until he'd successfully rebuilt the capillary system. With a sigh he gave the area a once over, noting the massive reduction in pain, and moved on.

The thigh wound was just as bad, if not worse. The healing sprays he'd used on the battlefield had sealed the wounds, Xaan's own physiology helping by slowing the blood flow to the area. That adaptation, one of the first the healers had made many years ago to the Latharian genetic code, had saved his life.

Sweat pouring from him, Laarn lost track of time as he worked through Xaan's wounds in sequence, starting with the thigh wound and ensuring that all the muscle fibers worked correctly and wouldn't adhere to each other before he moved on. It was no good saving a warrior's life if he couldn't fight. It would be more merciful to let him die, a call that Laarn had had to make in the past. But not now. Not today. Even if he took himself to the edge of exhaustion, he would ensure Xaandril would live to fight another day.

Hours later, he'd done just that as he sealed up the last of the minor wounds and left the bruising to heal on its own. As good as the technology was, he'd long ago learned to leave some things to heal in their own time. Otherwise things could go wrong. Almost like, once wounded, the body *needed* something to heal and if it couldn't find it, got confused and the immune system went into overdrive.

Satisfied he'd healed everything that was critical, he swept his focus over his patient once more and then disconnected with a sigh.

"Laarn to Draxx." He lifted his voice to trigger the comms system. "How far are we from Lathar Prime?"

As he waited for the commander's answer, he slumped against the support. Letting the assistants unbuckle him from the interface gauntlets, he flexed his fists as he drew his arms up to his chest. He was so hungry he could… what did Jess say? Ah, yes. He was so hungry, he could eat a horse. Halfway through the movement, he paused, his gaze riveted on his wrists.

There, wrapped around both like vines were dark marks.

Marks he'd only seen twice before in recent years. On his brother Tarrick, and his friend Karryl. Both warriors bonded to human females.

Bond marks.

The comm crackled as Draxx answered. *"Still a couple of hours out, my lord. How is the general?"*

"He'll live," Laarn answered shortly, his eyes wide as he studied his wrists. "But I suggest you take us to top speed and get us to the capital planet yesterday. We have a new problem."

HER WORLD HAD CHANGED FOREVER.

The next day Jess lay curled up in a bed in one of the private rooms off the main healer's hall. As soon as her pregnancy and the identity of the father had been confirmed, Tovan, the healer in charge of the hall in Laarn's absence, had refused to allow her to be moved due to her sickness. He and Daaynal had almost had a standup fight in the middle of the medbay over it, the smaller healer standing his ground and going toe to toe with the lethal emperor with determination written all over his face.

He wouldn't have won, not against Daaynal, and they all knew it but it was obvious he didn't care. Jess was his patient and what he said went. In the end though, Jess herself had stopped the fight by throwing up on the floor. Tovan had just looked at Daaynal pointedly and within an hour she'd been moved to a private room with a guard detail at the door.

She'd heard them talking when they thought she was asleep. She was the first woman to have become pregnant by a Lathar warrior in years, albeit it by unusual methods, and they weren't taking any chances. The guard detail on her door was just the start. There were more guards at all entrances to the healer's hall and Daaynal had increased the numbers in the palace.

But for the moment, she was alone, and for that she was grateful. It had taken most of the night for Tovan to stabilize her sickness, the tall, lean healer not leaving her side until he was sure she'd managed to keep some food and water down. Only then had he left her to rest and sought his own bed. She couldn't sleep though. Under the covers, her hand slid across her stomach.

Pregnant.

Even now, she couldn't believe it. The words—someone telling her she was pregnant, even seeing the results on screen, were one thing—but believing it, actually knowing deep in her heart, was another.

A baby.

Wonder filled her as her hand felt heavy against her stomach. Did it feel any different...rounder or harder perhaps? She'd never been pregnant before so she had no idea what to expect. She certainly hadn't been prepared for the wave of love and protectiveness that filled her at the thought of the tiny life nestled deep inside her womb. A baby. *Her* baby.

Laarn's baby.

She frowned, her heart clenching. She'd thought things were going well between them, and they had been. His kisses, his promises to make her his as soon as he got back... why would he do this? Impregnate her in secret, artificially... when they could have just done it the normal way? Hell, why hadn't he even *told* her? She rubbed at her forehead with shaking fingers. If he'd told her that he wanted a baby and the only way they could do it was through technology, she'd have understood. Been happy about it even. She'd always wanted a baby, provided she was with the child's father. So if he'd claimed her, or even promised to, before he put a baby in her belly, she'd have been happy.

Now? She was pregnant without nookie, and the father was nowhere to be seen. Apparently even Daaynal couldn't get hold of him. He was too busy with casualties on the front line. Jess dropped back on the pillows with a sigh and closed her eyes in exhaustion. Surely, he could spare a couple of minutes to answer an urgent message from his uncle, or even a minute to contact her to see how she was and let her know everything was going to be okay.

Perhaps he was lingering on the front line because he didn't want her...

A tear leaked from the corner of her eye and trailed down her cheek before she could stop it. As soon as she felt the wetness, she dashed it away in anger. What the fuck was she, a woman or a freaking mouse? She was pregnant, so fucking what? Her mom had been a single mom, bringing up twin daughters and a son. She had this, no father required. Especially not a handsome as hell, scarred up, healer who kissed like a sex god.

"Oh, my love... it breaks my heart to see you like this."

The male voice made her snap her eyes open to see Saal in the doorway, concern written on his face. Jess struggled to a sitting position, panic threading through her veins.

"Saal? What are you doing in here? The guards..."

"Hey, hey... you're perfectly safe, I assure you," he said, holding his hands out to the side as he approached. When she edged away, ready to swing her legs over the opposite side of the bed, he stopped dead.

"I would never hurt you, Jessica." His voice was low, his expression sincere. "As soon as I saw you, I wanted you. Even though you're carrying another male's child, I still want you."

"You have to leave. Please, Saal, you shouldn't be here. The emperor..." Now Daaynal knew she carried Laarn's child, he'd kill Saal for coming near her. And since all the guy had done was look after her, she couldn't allow that.

"Go, now, please?" she begged. Her voice was too weak, too thready as the adrenaline surging through her veins sapped her strength. "I couldn't bear it if you were hurt because of me."

His expression tightened for a moment, but then he nodded. "For you, my lady, anything. Just know I am never far away and if you need me, you only need mention it to your guard. Tinaas is a friend of mine. He will make sure a message gets to me..."

A sound in the corridor outside the room made him frown. Something about the way he turned and the set of his body sent alarm bells through her.

"What? What's wrong?"

The sound of laser fire outside the room answered her question and she sat bolt upright in bed. It wasn't right outside, but it sounded close. "Shit, what's going on?"

"I don't know," Saal answered. He was across the room and by her side in a heartbeat. "Can you walk?"

She nodded, taking his hand. "I'll damn well walk out of here."

"Good."

He supported her as she slid off the bed, arm ready to wrap around her waist in case she stumbled. She didn't, finding the strength from somewhere to lock her knees against the trembling. The fact that she only wore a sleep robe that bared most of her legs didn't bother her. Getting out of here before whoever was shooting got here very much did.

"Ready?" he asked when they reached the

doorway, a heavy pulse pistol in his free hand and a frown on his face as he looked down at her.

She took a deep breath, the movement making her feel queasy again but she fought it down to nod at him. "Yeah. What are you waiting for, a frigging invite?"

His lips quirked and he moved forward like he might kiss her. But she stopped him with an upraised hand. "Just try it, sweetheart, and mortal danger or not, my knee will be making friends with your crown jewels. Understand me?"

He did laugh at that. "Gods, you're gorgeous."

"Gorgeous and pregnant by someone else. Remember that and I won't have to separate you from your cock and balls. Now, I don't suppose you have a spare one of those, do you?"

He shook his head, moving closer to the door. One hand flat on the panel, he listened and then froze. "*Draanth...* they're right outside. Back... go back."

Before she knew what was happening, he hustled her backward, yanking open one of the doors on a cabinet.

"In," he ordered, cramming her into the small space so quickly her head caught on the top of the opening and her knee scraped against the side. She bit back her yelp, hearing the door to the room slide open a second after he'd shut the door on her.

She was trapped, in the dark, with only a thin piece of wood and a warrior she'd turned down between her and certain death.

She just had to hope it was enough.

11

"We're looking for the human breeder bitch," a rough voice announced, muffled slightly by the wood of the cabinet door. Jess held her breath, convinced they'd hear her frightened rasp even through it.

Saal gave a hard laugh, bitter and without mirth. "You're not the only one, brother. You with Dvarr too?"

There was a rumble, which she could only assume meant assent, because then Saal chuckled. "Yeah, I don't know who's with us or not either. He's playing his cards close to his chest. Can't blame him, though, not with what's at stake. The emperor, Terran-loving bastard he is, gets wind of this and we're all done for. I cleared this room... which ones have you done?"

Saal's voice faded along with the heavy footsteps and Jess sagged, leaning her forehead against the inside of the door in relief. He'd straight up saved her life. She dreaded to think what the purist warriors would have done if they'd found her in the room.

"Don't worry, little one," she whispered, her hand over her stomach. "You and me are getting out of this in one piece. I promise."

Holding her breath, she listened for any movement in the room outside the cupboard. Straining her ears for the slightest sound... the scuff of a boot across the floor, the whisper of leather clothing as it moved, even the whisper of air leaving lungs as someone breathed... but there was nothing. Relief had her breath slithering from her lungs in a rush as she pushed opened the door and unfolded herself from the cramped space.

Her stomach and heart fighting for space in her throat, she padded on silent feet to the door and listened out again. Silence met her ears so she risked sliding the door open and peeking out. If she had this wrong...

The corridor was empty. She didn't have time for relief though. At any moment, a warrior could come around the corner and she was trapped with nowhere to go and no weapon to fight back with.

Scooting around the door, she ran lightly down the corridor. First things first, she needed to find a weapons stash and arm up because until she did, she was a sitting duck. Sure, she might not have been a trained marine like Kenna and Jane, but she knew one end of a rifle from the other and her range scores had always been some of the highest on the base.

Three corridors later and the tension was beginning to mount, her shoulders riding higher as she expected at any moment to be shot between them. But each corridor was empty of both purist warriors and the recessed weapons lockers the octagonal ident tags around her neck would open.

"Shit, please tell me they have weapons in here..." she breathed to herself, reaching an intersection and going left. Left for Laarn, no other reason... which was probably as dumb as fuck but she couldn't stay still. With purist warriors searching for her, staying put was as good as a death sentence. She needed to keep on the move and just hope she was behind their sweeps. And that someone had thought to put weapons caches in the healer's hall.

They would, surely? For all this was a place of healing and... well, *not* violence and killing people, the Lathar were a warrior race. They even took their weapons into the damn toilet. She'd seen the stands.

Turning another corner, she spotted a locker on the wall, half hidden behind a support strut.

"*Thank fuck,*" she muttered under her breath and hurried toward it, yanking the ident tags from under her gown. The skin between her shoulder blades itched as the lock cycled and gave a loud ping as the lights on the front went green.

Shit, someone had to have heard that. Holding her breath, she tried to listen for the pounding of booted feet even as she yanked a weapons belt free. It was too large to go around her hips so she slid it over one shoulder, across her body and jammed a pulse-pistol into the holster.

Some of the rifles were too big, needing someone Laarn or Karryl's size to lift, so she grabbed one of the smaller ones, checking the charge as she'd been taught. It was fully loaded.

A grin on her lips, she turned and clicked the safety off. Let those purist bastards try to hurt her or her baby now.

Her footsteps were as loud as the breath in her lungs as she set off down the corridor. She'd not been in the "ward" area of the healer's hall before except for a brief tour from Laarn when they'd arrived. So she operated on the vague memory of a central area containing the labs, with corridors leading off it like spokes of a wheel. A big main corridor had circled the entire hall with smaller corridors running parallel to it.

Guessing that the purists would likely be holding the main corridor, she ducked into one of the smaller ones, working her way through, maze like, until she figured she was somewhere near the main labs and medbay... and, more importantly, the main door out of the place.

"Got to be the only planet in the fucking universe to stick the damn hospital in the fucking basement," she groused under her breath. Running on light feet to the end of the corridor, she risked a quick look around the corner and quickly ducked back into cover.

There were two warriors covering the main lab. She hissed lightly between her teeth as she considered her options. She was alone behind enemy lines and she'd just become purist public enemy number one. She'd managed to avoid running into any of them so far but she wasn't delusional enough to think her luck would hold out much longer.

Casting a glance back the way she'd come, she nibbled her lip. Should she double back and try and find another way out? There had to be service ducts or something, maybe even maintenance shafts, she could use. Hell, she'd even settle for the old movie staple of ventilation shafts right about now.

Decision made, she took three steps away from the corner when she heard it. Boots. Heavy ones. Not from the two men in the lab in front of her, but in the corridors back the way she'd come. Freezing in place, she listened. Her finger slid off the trigger guard and curled around the trigger as she lifted the rifle into her shoulder. That was more than one man, and they were getting louder. The question was, would they come this way or turn off to search one of the subsidiary corridors?

A couple more seconds and her question was answered as the boots got louder. They were past the secondary corridor junction and were headed right for her. Which meant she had only two options left —face however many of them turned the corner in a moment...

Or take on the two men in the lab.

She cursed under her breath and turned on her heel. Fast steps took her to the corner and she barreled around it before she could think how fucking dumb this was.

As soon as she cleared the corner, she started firing, cutting down the first guard in a hail of laser bolts. Rapid fire, close grouping, just as she'd been trained and the man lurched, his body dancing and jerking before dropping like a puppet with its strings cut.

Jess didn't blink, firing at the other warrior as he dived for cover. She might not have been the dyed in the wool, born for war marine Jane and Kenna were, but when her life... her baby's life... was on the line she could and would kill with the best of them.

Shouts sounded behind her, but she ignored them in favor of darting across the lab, keeping her enemy's head down with covering fire as she approached his position, crouched behind one of the big diagnostic beds.

He tried to dart out of cover to fire at her, but each time his head broke cover, the movement was met with a burst of rapid fire. Before she'd made it halfway across the room, she heard the rifle, designed for the Lathar method of accurate with one round at a time shooting, begin to overload. Grinning like a fool, she rattled off a couple more bursts and then threw the thing over-arm.

It tumbled through the air, the whine from the overloading power pack getting louder and louder. Diving to the side, she took cover behind another bed as the rifle clattered into the wall then hit the floor. The warrior crouching there managed a small curse, the slide of leather and the thump of boots sounding as he tried to get clear.

BOOM!

The blast shook the walls as the rifle went critical and exploded. Her ears ringing, Jess was on her feet in an instant, staggering toward the frosted glass double doors at the front of the medbay. Red lights to one side warned her that the assholes had locked it. With her eyes streaming and warriors about to pour into the room behind her, she didn't have time to stop and unlock it. Instead, she grabbed for the pistol in the holster at her side and, holding it in both hands, aimed at the doors.

As she pulled the trigger, she sent a prayer up to anyone who might be listening.

Please don't let the bloody doors be bulletproof...

The instant the shuttle touched down, Laarn was at the airlock door, waiting for it to cycle so he could get off the damn thing. He'd showered and changed since he'd come out of surgery, but sleep had eluded him. How could he sleep with mating marks around his wrists? Marks he'd dreamed of being called forward in his skin all his life, but that shouldn't… couldn't be there, not yet.

Even he didn't understand the mechanism but marks were only called to a male's skin after he'd claimed his woman… or something else happened. Since he hadn't claimed Jess' delectable, curvy little body for his own yet, that left something else.

The thought of what else it could possibly be had his heart thudding against his chest in fear as the door finally opened and he bolted through it. He cleared the ramp in one leap, his booted feet hitting the flagstones of the landing pad hard, but he was already running.

One of the reasons that could call marks to a male's skin was the death, or near death of the female he longed to claim. Fear gripped him as he pounded through the corridors of the palace, heading for the healer's hall. If anything had happened to Jess, that's where she'd be... He growled in frustration... in the care of second-rate healers while he, the best of them, had been on the front line, far away from the woman he...

He couldn't complete the thought, a frown on his face as he realized he wasn't the only person running toward the healer's hall. Two full squads of warriors ran down the opposite side of one of the many galleries on the way. Sure enough, as soon as he noticed them, the palace alarms started blaring.

"Hey!" he called out, altering direction to intercept the squad. "What's happening?"

"Lord Healer." Somehow the warrior at the front of the group managed to incline his head and give the impression of a bow while running at full tilt. "Purists in the palace. They've sealed themselves in the sickbay with one of the human females."

"Draanth!" Laarn burst out, exhaustion and fear robbing him of his normal poise. "Which one?"

"The little one... Lady Kallson?"

Nononono... Not his Jess.

Laarn managed to keep his horrified moan to himself and upped his pace, his long stride leaving even the fastest of the warriors in his wake as he sped toward the healer's hall. Making it in record time, he all but slid around the last corner and found the corridor in front of the entrance to the healer's hall packed.

Warriors thronged around the double doors, voices raised in frustration as different people tried to make themselves heard. In the middle of it all stood Daaynal, a dark expression on his face as he obviously lost his patience and bellowed.

"SILENCE!"

All the voices fell silent, and every pair of eyes turned toward the warrior emperor. He gestured to the doors. "Get those damn doors open. I don't care how. Blow them out of the wall if you have to, but get them open."

"That won't work," Laarn cut in, jostling through the crowds to reach his uncle's side. "The hall is designed as a last redoubt if the palace is breached. It's built to withstand even a *drakeen* assault."

"*Draanth!*" Daaynal hissed. "Why the *fuck* wasn't I informed of that?"

Laarn blinked at his adoption of the human word. If the situation weren't so critical, he might even have smiled and teased his uncle at his forward thinking. As it was, he just shrugged.

"The hall has secrets only the lord healer and his men need to know. The ability to guard the Arc is one of them," he said, naming the central computer and storage core buried deep in the earth below both the palace and the healer's hall.

An ancient installation, it housed the entirety of the Lathar knowledge of genetic manipulation and samples going back thousands of years. It was said that somewhere in the archives was their original genetic code, but the modern systems only went so far back and the older archives were perilous and unsafe to venture into.

"The front doors, you see," he continued, "are backed up by force fields and a vibrational-energy molecular shield. Fire on it, even with an energy pistol and it will return the yield tenfold. Which, given the close confines of this corridor, will kill anyone in here. The *only* way to shoot out the doors is from inside."

"NO ONE FIRE ON THOSE DOORS!" Daaynal bellowed, stopping at least three warriors from doing just that. He returned his attention to Laarn, his expression steely. "When this is over, you *are* going to tell me everything I don't know about the hall."

"Maybe. If you tell me what the *draanth* is going on. Purists in the palace? Again?" he demanded, not caring that he'd just snapped at the emperor himself.

"We were watching a cell, preparing to move in to try and get the leaders, but they moved unexpectedly." Daaynal reached out, using a big hand on Laarn's arm to hustle him to one side.

"Is there any other way in?" he asked in a low, urgent voice. "We *need* to get Miss Kallson out. She's..." Pausing, he looked at Laarn curiously. "You're taking this very well for a male in your position. If that were my female in there in that condition..."

"A male in my position? What do you mean?" Sudden wariness rolled through Laarn and his hand stilled where he'd been about to pull his sleeve back and show his uncle the dark marks around his wrists.

"She's pregnant," Daaynal said bluntly.

Shock and then pain lanced through Laarn, and he couldn't stop the quick inward breath. "We haven't..." he started, his words trailing off under the assault of the thoughts tumbling through his head.

Had he missed his chance with her? Had she taken another male as mate while he'd been gone... His expression hardened. He'd *told* her she was his, that as soon as he got back he'd claim her fully...

She'd given him her pleasure, writhing on his fingers as he'd made her come.

"*Faithless female,*" he hissed, drawing his lips back from his teeth, but Daaynal held his hand up, shaking his head.

"No, we had the baby's genetics tested. It's either yours or Tarrick's, and I'm fairly sure your *litaan* has his hands too full with his mate to claim another female."

The baby. His baby. *His* child.

For a moment Laarn couldn't breathe, couldn't think as the thoughts tumbled through his mind. He was going to be a father... an honor that he'd never thought he'd achieve.

And she was locked in the hall with purists...

"We need to get in there. Now."

"Way to go, Captain Obvious," Daaynal threw back, making Laarn's lips quirk. Seemed someone else had been as fascinated with the Terrans as he and his brother-warriors had. "How do you sugg—"

Before he could finish the sentence, the sound of shots rang out. Both Laarn and Daaynal whipped their heads around, the admonishment already on Laarn's lips not to shoot at the damn doors when both realized the shots had come from within the hall itself.

"What the…"

Like the rest of the men in the hall, they turned toward the glass doors. The shots were muffled, but they could all see the muzzle flashes as a rifle fired repeatedly on the other side. Laarn shot a look at Daaynal, who looked puzzled.

"Human soldiers shoot like that," he explained. "Rapid fire in bursts. We saw it when the T'Laat tried to take them. They bottlenecked a corridor and blew the *draanth* out of them. The T'Laat didn't know what hit them, especially when the rifles started to overload."

"And?" Daaynal demanded.

"They used them as explosives." As soon as he said the words, Laarn knew what Jess was going to do. They couldn't open the doors from this side, but if she had weaponry…

"CLEAR THE DOORS," he shouted. "GET READY TO MOVE AS SOON AS THEY'RE DOWN!"

The whine from the other side of the glass was followed by a clatter, then…

BOOM!

The explosion lit the glass up in a flare of green and gold, so bright the warriors in the corridor had to look away. Before the sound had cleared, there were more shots... two dull thuds on the other side of the glass doors as something hit them. Then they cracked, shattering into a million pieces to spill out over the floor of the corridor, leaving a gaping hole filled with smoke.

Bloodied and pale, his little Jess stepped through the gap, a pistol held in a no-nonsense grip. She looked at them and blinked, shaking her head.

"YOU MIGHT WANNA GET IN THERE..." she shouted and then shook her head, stepping aside as warriors poured through the gap behind her. "Crap, sorry... hearing's shit at the moment. Purists, in the corridors right behind me. Led by a guy called Dvarr apparently."

Daaynal snarled, anger evident on his face, but Laarn was done talking. Moving in, he pulled her into his arms. She nestled against him with a soft sigh, her hands on his chest as he plucked the pistol from her, handing it off to a warrior behind her and holding her tightly as sheer relief rolled through him.

"Gods, little one. I thought I'd lost you," he murmured against her hair.

Fear the like of which he'd never known had run through him at the thought of her dead or dying, the light in her lovely eyes snuffed out forever. He'd never felt such fear or emotion before, and it humbled him. Somehow, she'd gotten under his skin and become his reason for breathing, for being... for everything.

Closing his eyes, he let the feelings wash over and through him. For the first time in his life he felt... complete. Content. She fit into a place in his heart he hadn't realized was empty. Moving his head, he placed a gentle kiss against her temple, not caring that they were in the middle of a crowded corridor and everyone would see him. As a human would say, fuck them, let them look. She was his and he wanted everyone to know it.

Murmuring, she pulled away and he looked down at her, reluctant to let her go from his embrace. Her expression was taut and angry, giving him a moment's warning before she wound her arm back and punched him in the jaw.

Pain radiated through the side of his face and he blinked, rocking back on his heels a little as he absorbed the blow. It was a good one, delivered well and by someone who had obviously been taught to punch.

"My love?" he murmured, confused. She'd been happy to see him. He *knew* she had. Why else would she cling to him the way she had? "Is there a problem?"

"That's for knocking me up without fucking asking," she hissed. "Or even fucking. Fucking or asking, either would have been a good thing, don't you think?"

12

Fury joined the merry party of adrenaline and relief surging through Jess' system. She couldn't believe she'd made it to safety, against the odds, but that light-headedness flipped to something darker as she looked at Laarn, standing in front of her as bold as brass, saying he'd been scared he would lose her. Her hand stole down to cover her stomach. Asshole hadn't even *had* her yet, so how could he lose her?

Ignoring the small gasps and interested silence from the crowd around them, she held his gaze, refusing to look away. A challenge, something they'd been warned not to do with any of the warriors, but right now she didn't care. This could develop into a full on bitching out fest and she wouldn't care a jot.

Let the rest of them see that their fucking holier than thou lord healer was a man just like them. *Him* included.

"Talk," she advised. "And talk fast."

His gaze never left hers. "My love, I can explain. Let's take this somewhere else and we'll talk?"

Her lip curled back. "Don't you fucking *my love* me. How about you explain right here."

His eyes flickered to the side, the implacable mask slipping for a moment. "We're not alone..."

"Oh, I realize that." Jess laughed. If she'd been herself and people hadn't been trying to kill her for the last hour or so, she'd have winced at the harsh sound. She didn't. Instead, she folded her arms in a silent signal that she was going precisely nowhere and he'd be a fool to try and make her.

"Just as I wasn't alone when your healer basically called me a slut when I didn't know who the father of my baby was...."

The memory of the condemning look on Tovan's face was imprinted on her mind forever. The half second of disgust that slid into speculation before he'd covered it all up with the professional doctor's face, but she'd seen it. Known what he was thinking. That if she'd slept with so many Lathar that she didn't know who'd fathered her child, perhaps he had a chance of getting between her thighs.

"...a baby I had *no* idea I was having because I haven't had sex with anyone since I left Earth. And for humans, there has to be some cock in cunt action for conception to take place. You see where I'm going with this?" she demanded, not caring that he winced at her foul language. He'd knocked her up without so much as a by-your-leave... she had a right to be a little pissy about the situation.

"Jess, please understand. I didn't mean for this to happen." He stepped toward her as though to pull her into his arms again.

Tears thickening the back of her throat, she stepped back with a glare, wishing she hadn't given up her pistol so easily. Now the excitement from nearly getting killed by purists was wearing off, her control and emotions were on a knife-edge. One touch from him and she'd crack, burst into tears and ruin her tough-girl image.

"What *did* you mean to happen then?" she demanded, trying for sharp but managing hurt instead. The sound of the pain in her own voice widened the cracks in her shields and just like that, they began to crumble.

"I thought we had an agreement... an

understanding? If you'd wanted a baby *that* badly we could've just... yeah. If you'd wanted to make *sure,* that would have been cool too but..." She coughed, trying to cover the lump in the back of her throat, but it was no good. The tears had already begun to leak.

With a muffled curse, he was on her, hauling her back into his embrace with strong hands. Drawing in a shuddering breath, she didn't fight. She couldn't. She couldn't fight him and the tears that threatened to overwhelm her.

"I mean... it's no secret that I had a thing for you. Right from the beginning I'd hoped that if any warrior claimed me, it would be you, even if you did glare all the time and try and scare me off."

He lifted her chin, wiping her tears with gentle fingers.

"Shhh... we did, we *do* have an agreement," he said in a soft rumble, his green eyes locked onto hers, his stare intense. "And I didn't intend for this to happen. Do you think I would have denied myself your body and your pleasure in favor of getting you with child through other means? Yes, I took your eggs and fertilized them to see if my theory was correct. *But,* I didn't implant them. I swear on my oath as a healer, Jess, I would never do that to you."

He leaned down to brush his lips over hers and she shivered, closing her eyes as she fought the need to surrender to him.

"Jess, did you go into my lab for anything while I was gone?" he asked, lifting her chin up so she had to meet his eyes.

She frowned. "Errr... yeah. I didn't feel well and none of the other healers seemed interested in talking to me so I tried your lab. It let me in, though, and I didn't touch anything, I swear. Just used the diagnostic bed, that's all," she assured him earnestly.

Crap. What if there was a penalty for trespassing in the labs or if she'd destroyed a delicate experiment or something? Then she winced as she realized she'd not only destroyed *all* the experiments, but the labs to boot. If there had been anything delicate in there, it was a shattered, twisted mess now.

But, unexpectedly, he smiled. "That explains it, my love. I didn't destroy the eggs. They were stored in my lab. When you initiated treatment, the AI must have thought you wanted to implant them and did."

She looked at him for long moments, replaying what she remembered of her visit in her head. "It did mention something about viable tests and if I wanted to proceed." Her cheeks burned as she realized how stupid she sounded, adding in a small voice. "I thought it just meant proceed with treatment for my stomach bug. Then my abdomen got hot, but much lower down than for a digestive problem."

The backs of his fingers brushed gently against her cheek. "That was the implantation sequence, my love."

There was a cough behind them and they both turned to find Daaynal looking down at them. "Laarn, I think it may be better if you took the Lady Jessica to the safety of your quarters while we deal with this situation here."

Laarn inclined his head. "Of course, Your Majesty. Immediately."

She bit her lip as he bent to scoop her up, her skirts rustling around her legs in a swish of silk as he held her high against his chest like she was the most delicate thing in the universe. The leather of his jacket was warm beneath her fingers as she wrapped her arm around his shoulders. Not to hold on, he would never have dropped her, but because she wanted to touch him. Reaching out, she wound her fingers through his hair, savoring the feel of the silky locks against her skin.

"Wait!"

Laarn had barely taken two steps when a harsh voice rang out from behind them. He half turned, Jess peeking from around him, to see Saal in the ruins of the lab doorway. A rifle in one hand and a blade in the other, it was obvious from his bloodstained face he'd been in a hard-won fight.

"I challenge Laarn K'Vass," he announced, pointing at the healer with the big knife in his hand. "For the right to claim Lady Jessica of Earth."

"No."

Laarn's snarl was instinctive. Jess was *his*. Even if she weren't carrying his baby, she would have been soon anyway. And she would be again. Soon. As soon as she birthed this one, he planned on putting another in her belly, the traditional way.

"She's mine. She's accepted my claim. She carries my child."

He didn't miss the flash of anger at his words, particularly the last ones. Of course, he knew Saal had been sniffing around Jess for weeks, but she hadn't paid him any mind, avoiding him wherever she could. The fact that the male had kept up his pursuit, despite no signs of interest from the female he wanted, said he was both too stubborn and too stupid for his own good.

"Your Majesty," Saal spoke directly to Daaynal, who was watching the scene with a big shoulder leaned against the corridor wall and his arms folded. His expression was so forbidding Laarn probably wouldn't have addressed him directly, even though he was the guy's sister-son.

"This warrior," Saal indicated Laarn, "left his mate unattended and in danger. *I* protected her. Therefore, by our laws I have the right to challenge his claim on her."

"That's a load of *trall*," Laarn snapped, irritated beyond measure that this piece of *draanth* was even still speaking. There was no way he was letting a little fucking upstart, a lowly J'Qess, steal his little human from under his nose. "Jess protected herself. We all saw it."

"Not when they attacked she didn't," Saal argued. "They came to her room first and she'd be dead, or worse, if I hadn't hidden her."

Daaynal turned his head. "Lady Jessica, is this true?"

Jess nodded, her face pale, and Laarn growled in anger. "It means nothing. He's just trying to cover his ass. We all know he was friends with Dvarr. I say we execute him, here and now, for purist leanings."

"No! He's not!" Jess burst out, her arm tightening around his neck. She looked at him, her full bottom lip quivering just a little. "He's not Dvarr's friend. He's saved me from him before when he was guarding the emperor's war-room. I wanted to see you..." she said to Daaynal. "About my twin sister, the ill one? But he wouldn't let me in. Threatened me. Saal saved me then as well."

Daaynal sighed, running a hand through his long hair. "Well, that does put us in a bit of a bind, doesn't it? If he's protected your female twice, Laarn, then he *does* have the right to challenge."

"No..." Jess gasped, clinging tightly to him. Her horror at the idea eased something deep in his chest. "But I don't want him, Saal that is. I mean, I'm grateful to him for rescuing me, but I don't want him as my husband... err, mate. Laarn is my mate."

"Not yet," Daaynal growled as he pushed off from the wall. "Laarn, Lord Healer... do you accept the challenge?"

"Gladly." He let go of Jess' knees and stood her on her feet, pushing her gently behind him. "I'll make him wish he'd never been fucking born."

"You can try, *healer*," Saal spat the word like a

curse, throwing the rifle to the side as he advanced. Tension in the corridor rose as warriors moved out of the way, lining the walls to watch. It was rare a warrior of Laarn's standing was challenged, and the lord healer to boot? This would be all around the palace before sundown.

Laarn grinned as he pulled the big sword from its sheath between his shoulders and paced around his opponent, stalking him like a *deearin* stalking its prey. Unlike some warriors, he had none of the big feline DNA in his genetic makeup, but he felt like it now, his eyes narrowing as he focused on the fight ahead.

Although Saal was from a lower ranked clan, that didn't mean he wasn't a good fighter. His position as war commander, albeit of a very small group, stood testament to that, as did his steady gaze and firm grip on the weapon in his hand.

Laarn's amusement fell away as they sized each other up. Neither of them made a move, not yet, too concerned with watching how the other moved, the way he gripped his weapon. Neither was inexperienced enough to think this was an idle or easy bout.

Saal was the first to move, using the big, vicious-looking blade in his hand to test Laarn's defenses.

Shorter and wider, it wasn't as refined as the blade Laarn wielded but more brutal, designed for messy, close-quarters combat.

The healer blocked instantly, knocking the blade aside, and sneered. "Is that all you got? A child could fight better."

At his taunt, Saal snarled and attacked in a rush. Laarn met him with a bellow of his own, their blades clashing in midair. Saal grinned, twisting his blade and trying to snare Laarn's up, but he'd been in too many battles to be fooled by such a trick, slamming his elbow up into Saal's face.

The other warrior grunted, jerking his head back so only the edge of Laarn's elbow grazed his jaw. They broke apart, circling again. The next time, Laarn attacked first in a flurry of heavy blows designed to drive his opponent back. In a challenge fight, it would be to the edge of the area and out of it, but today? He planned to pin the bastard to the bulkhead with his own weapon.

Saal kept blocking, so Laarn kept moving, kept driving forward. His hair danced over his shoulders, his body in constant movement as he used the powerful muscles in his torso to make the big blade twist and turn in a deadly dance of flashing steel.

Saal blocked, time after time, but Laarn didn't

care, his focus absolute. With each clash of blades, the younger warrior got a little sloppier, a little slower... slow enough to start leaving openings in his defense.

Laarn grinned, an evil expression that had nothing to do with humor, and slid a jab into the next opening he saw. Then a solid kick into the next. Each time Saal left himself open, Laarn capitalized on it. But not with his blade. Oh no, that would be too quick and he wanted this asshole to bleed... to *suffer*... to stand as a warning to every other warrior out there that Jessica Kallson was *his*.

Instead, he took Saal apart with his fists, switching his blade from hand to hand to keep the male's dagger at bay as he got a blow through every gap he could. Blood dripped to the floor as they moved, splattering across the bulkhead with each heavy blow. Saal's blocks got weaker and weaker, the male stumbling backward and desperately blocking. Fear showed stark on his face, his arms trembling as he tried to lift his blade one last time.

Laarn growled and slapped the weak block aside, reaching in to wrench the blade from Saal's grip. Throwing both their weapons aside with a clatter, he grabbed the other male by the throat and pinned him against the wall, his feet dangling inches off the floor.

"Jess is *mine*," he hissed right in Saal's face.

Saal's face was bruised and bloody, one eye already swollen shut... he needed a healer but Laarn didn't care. It wasn't going to be him, that was for sure.

"Touch her again, think about touching her... gods, you even *look* at her the wrong way, and I'll fucking gut you... slowly. Over days." He smiled deliberately. "If I can bring a warrior back from the grip of death, how long do you think I can make you dance on its edge? Think about it."

Letting go, he watched as Saal dropped in a pathetic heap on the floor. Without another word, he turned and walked toward Jess. She watched him with wide eyes as he came to a stop in front of her. He was bloody from the fight, but he didn't care. If she wanted him, she had to accept all of him. Lifting his hand, he held it out.

"Lady Jessica, do you accept my claim?"

13

As soon as she'd said yes, Laarn had scooped her up in his arms and carried her in silence through the warriors lining the walls of the corridor. A walk of triumph, he'd made sure to look each warrior in the eye as they passed, the hard, possessive look on his face making Jess shiver.

Silence had reigned on the walk back to his quarters. A feeling of safety filled her as she curled up next to his broad chest, her arms around his neck, but she was tempered with increasing anticipation and nervousness when he didn't speak.

She stole a look at his face, their gazes clashing. His expression was tight, not the pleasant and neutral one she was used to seeing. A shiver rolled down her spine. She'd spent weeks pushing him, trying to get under his guard and now that she had, she had the sudden feeling she'd poked the bear once too often.

Since she'd first met him, she'd wondered what an enraged Laarn would be like, and she'd seen it in the corridor outside the healer's hall as he'd practically taken Saal apart with his bare hands.

She'd seen many fights in her time—growing up in a crowded tower habitat, illegal bareknuckle fights for money and gang clashes over territory had been commonplace—and only an idiot would have thought Laarn had needed the big sword back in place over his shoulders to take Saal down.

Instead, the weapon had been merely window dressing. Seconds in, it had been apparent that Saal was out of his depth—outweighed and outmatched by the tall, rangy healer. Laarn's attacks had been methodical and precise, that of a surgeon as he targeted his blows for maximum effectiveness. Another shiver hit her. She'd always seen the kind and gentle side of Laarn—kind and gentle for a Lathar anyway—but today she'd seen the warrior and he was awe inspiring.

And deadly.

All to claim her.

She bit her lip as they turned another corner.

They were in a part of the palace she'd never been to, one of the western wings and she started to take notice. Although she knew Laarn had to have quarters of his own here, she'd only ever seen him at the lab, even when it was obvious he'd just woken up.

Less than a minute later, he stopped before a set of double doors, which slid open silently in front of them. As he carried her inside, her eyes widened at the opulence of the rooms, quickly glimpsed as he carried her through to a huge bedroom. The decor wasn't the clean, white and marble utilitarian sort she had grown used to seeing. Instead, it was all heavy wood and embroidered drapes, an older style, which made her think of a nomad tent or a desert sheikh's harem.

Laarn didn't stop until they were standing next to the canopied bed, still holding her in his arms as he looked directly into her eyes.

"A better man would give you a choice here," he said, his deep voice low. "A chance to change your mind about my claim and leave if you prefer Sa..." He paused on the name, his lip curling slightly. "A chance to leave and find the warrior I bested. But I am not that man," he snarled, his grip tightening. "You're mine now, Jess, and I'll never let you go. I ache to claim you, to finally make you mine, in every sense of the word."

A thrill shot through her body at his words, arousal and anticipation working their seductive spell. He bent down, placing her on her feet carefully. Too carefully, his entire frame solid with tension.

Standing straight, he looked down at her, his expression unreadable.

"Take the gown off, or by all the gods, I'll fucking tear it off."

She hardly recognized his voice, harsh and guttural. The sudden look on his face, hard and feral, sent a wave of fear through her. Instinctively, she backed up a step, nerves setting in.

Instantly, fury flared across his features and within a second he was on her, his big hand capturing the back of her neck in an iron grip. His eyes glittered.

"Oh no, sweetheart. You don't get to run. Not now. Not after this."

A cry escaped her as he yanked her toward him, his free hand catching on the front of her gown. With a savage yank, he tore it clean down the middle, baring her naked body beneath to his gaze. Frozen, she looked up at him as his eyes slid down her, the hard look in them dissolving into heat as they paused on the swell of her breasts.

He stopped dead, his hand still on the back of her neck as he made a slow perusal of her body. She bit her lip, worry filling her. She'd pushed him to claim her, but what did he think now that he saw her body for the first time? Did he like what he saw... she wasn't model thin, nor toned and fit like Jane or Kenna. She was just... average.

He looked down further, over the stomach she tried to suck in, those last few pounds she could never get rid of no matter how long she spent on the treadmill or how many sit-ups she tortured herself with showing there. The hard look on his face dissolved into heat as his gaze swept down her bare legs and then back up to settle at the juncture to her thighs. She resisted the urge... the need... to press her legs together as she remembered his clever fingers on her clit, in her pussy, as she'd ridden him to orgasm. She'd been able to tell he was a surgeon then, his hands dexterous and agile.

He released her and nodded toward the bed.

"On there. On your back... legs spread."

His voice was still unrecognizable—a rough growl. Instinctively, she moved toward him, craving something... anything. Some sort of softness or tenderness to reassure her that she hadn't made a horrible mistake.

"*Do it, Jessica,*" he snapped, his hands tearing at his weapons belt and jacket. "I'm too close to the edge for you to fight me, little one."

His voice broke on the last word and her eyes widened, sudden understanding filling her as she glimpsed past his implacable mask and saw the stark fear and need there. She'd scared him, badly.

Stepping back, she let the remnants of her dress slip from her shoulders. He watched her like a hawk, his hands stilling for a moment on his belt as he undid it, like he couldn't bear to look away. Like she was the only thing in the universe for him as she moved. Heat flared in his gaze again, and his hand shook as he tore at his buckle.

A surge of power filled her as soon as she saw it. Feminine pride and the knowledge that he was *hers,* that the sight of her naked body held him enthralled, rolled through her as she stepped back. Her movements were as seductive as she could make them as she slid backward onto the bed. Lying back, she kept her knees together for a moment, arching her back and body to show it off to best advantage as she slid her hands through her hair.

Settling back, she caught his gaze and then

parted her thighs for him.

He was still watching her, his eyes narrowed but at his side, his jaw clenched and unclenched, the knuckles showing white.

"Touch yourself," he ordered, shoving his pants down off his hips. "I want to see how you pleasure yourself. What you like. Make yourself wet for me."

She nodded, unable to speak, and slid her hand down the front of her body to dip between her legs. As her fingers grazed her clit, his cock popped free, arching tall and proud up toward his flat, muscled stomach. A small gasp left her lips. He was huge and thick, far bigger than she'd thought.

Fisting his cock, he stroked. The broad, flushed head slick with precum played peek-a-boo with his hand as he stepped out of his pants and boots, but his eyes never left her, riveted to her fingers between her legs.

She played with her clit, using her other hand to part her pussy lips as she circled and stroked. She teased the small bud into a hard little nubbin and then rolled her fingertip over the beaded pearl. Her breathing shortened, her hips rocking as she remembered how he'd touched her. How much she'd liked it. How he'd made her come, hard and fast.

"Stop," he ordered when she was almost there, her body straining for release. She did, instantly, locking her gaze with his as he moved to kneel on the bed—one knee, then the other, his cock still in his hand. He knelt between her parted thighs, stroking his cock as he looked down on her with a possessive gaze.

"Hands up, above your head." His chest heaved, breathing short, and each word had a little growl on the end. Wordlessly, she obeyed, putting her hands either side of her head and watching him. Waiting for his next move.

With a growl, he braced himself over her, cock in hand and she tensed, anticipating the press of his hot flesh into hers. He moved, and she jumped as his fingers swept through her folds. His lips grazed over hers. Would he take her hard and fast, claiming her in one thrust? Was that why he'd had her pleasure herself, make herself wet for him?

"*Mine.*"

The word was growled against her lips and then he was gone, sliding down her body. She whimpered as he parted her thighs roughly, wedging his broad shoulders between them. His breath washed over her pussy lips and she tensed. His tongue rasped over her, warm and wet. Her hips jerked off the bed, a soft keen falling from her lips. It was met by a deep growl and his hands closing around her thighs, holding her still as he licked her again. Found her clit.

Sucked.

Hard.

Her head thrashed on the bed as he set about driving her out of her mind. Forget clever fingers, the man had a gifted tongue. She writhed, or tried to, as he took her with his mouth. Licking and suckling at her clit like a man starved before thrusting his tongue deep within to collect every drop of her arousal. Moans slipped from her lips as he brought her near the edge quickly and ruthlessly, her hands moving down so she could slide her fingers through his long hair.

He reacted instantly, tearing from her in an explosion of movement. Grabbing her hands, he surged over her, slamming them back into the bed above her head and holding them there.

"I said, *hands up*," he growled, flicking his hair to one side, over his shoulder as he transferred both her wrists to one hand. She nodded, breath coming in short pants as he kept her thighs apart with a hard knee. She'd do whatever he wanted, if he didn't stop touching her. He wouldn't hurt her, she knew that without thinking, but this rough, near ruthless side of him, a side she hadn't expected, turned her on like nothing else.

Reaching between them, he brought the thick head of his cock to bear against the entrance to her pussy. She bit her lip, sucking in a hard breath as he pushed, breaching her in one hard movement and seating himself to the hilt.

"Oh, shit..." she moaned, her back arched as she was filled suddenly, his thick cock stretching her inner walls to capacity. It burned. But felt *so* good. "Yes, please, yes."

He groaned, his eyes half closed and his lips parted as his cock throbbed within her, but then he pulled back. Thrust again. Hard and fast. Their moans mingled in the air as he did it again, setting up a hard and fast rhythm.

She gave herself up to pleasure and him, arching her back and rocking her hips to match each of his thrusts. There was no finesse about his love-making now, just raw power as he claimed her. Each rock of his hips drove his cock deep inside her, each grind of his pelvis against hers trapping her clit between them and sending waves of pleasure through her.

"Laarn," she gasped, pulling on her wrists in his hold. "Please... I want..."

He nodded, his hair brushing her cheeks as he leaned down to claim her lips in a torrid kiss. His tongue thrust into her mouth in concert with his cock in her cunt, but he let go of her hands. She wrapped her arms around his neck, kissing him back as he took her. He claimed her in hard thrusts, each one a declaration that she belonged to him, and only him.

Then it was all too much. The tension in her body, in her pussy clenched tightly around him, was all too much. Her movements faltered, hips jerking as she came, crying out into his mouth as he claimed her pleasure as well as her body.

Wave after wave of bliss drenched her body like the waves of the ocean. She whimpered and clung to him, her eyes pressed shut as he sped up, the near-frantic pace of his hard strokes driving her higher.

Then he broke from her lips with a groan, slammed into her a last time and stiffened. She moaned as she felt him come, hard and hot, deep inside her. She held him tightly, hand in his hair at the back of his neck. If she hadn't already been pregnant, there was no way she wouldn't have been now.

She was his.

14

Jess was incredible. Utterly amazing. Her hot little body clenched tightly around his cock as he'd taken her over and over was everything Laarn had dreamed it would be and more. Much more.

But as hot as the sex was, lying next to her as she slept, feeling her pliant and trusting in his arms... *That* had been the stuff his deepest, darkest, wouldn't admit to anyone on pain of death fantasies had been.

Lying there with her sleeping in his arms, he'd held her close, sliding a hand over her still flat stomach. Wonder still filled him that she carried his child safely within her and that moment, that memory of holding her, would forever be etched in his memory.

The knowledge that he wouldn't be alone as he lived out his life... the fact he had a female by his side as his partner, to bear his children, had finally sunk in and had he been standing, would have brought him to his knees.

She was his, his mate, his life... An *intelligent* female, not a near animal like the oonat some of his brothers had settled for, but a real woman with wit and intelligence who he could have a conversation with.

He re-entered his, no *their* quarters with an excitement rolling through his veins he hadn't felt for years coming through those doors because he knew she waited for him within.

His cock, semi-hard all day, flared to life and pressed uncomfortably against the front of his leathers. He was as stiff as a flagpole, even though he'd had her more times than he could count last night and then again before he'd left this morning. Leaving her all sleepy and sated in his bed, her lips plump from his kisses, had been the hardest thing he'd ever done.

But now he was back, and the hours he'd spent

in the lab were too many away from her and the haven of her sweet body.

"Jess?" he called out, not finding her in the cool shade of the main rooms. Like most Latharian summers, the day was hot enough to burn flesh from bones, the heat only just starting to dissipate as the sun neared the horizon.

"Jessica?" He looked into the bedroom, not finding her sleeping either.

A pang of disappointment hit him. One of his favorite parts from last night had been rousing her from sleep so he could take her again. She'd seemed to particularly like his tongue against her clit, her little toes curling as she came back to wakefulness with a feline stretch that quickly turned into a hoarse scream as she came.

Panic replaced the disappointment, though, as he couldn't find her in the facilities either, but then the soft splash of water from outside got his attention. The bathing pool. A groan whispered from his lips at the thought of her naked in the silky water.

"*Draanth...*" he breathed, his cock jerking savagely. He had to have her again.

Striding out onto the veranda, he stopped short at the side before him. In this, one of the older parts of the Imperial palace, the quarters were larger and more ornate, which extended outside as well. His bathing pool ran the length of the veranda, the cool water reflecting the blue tiles beneath invitingly. But no water could be as inviting as the woman floating on her back in the middle, as naked as the day she'd been born. Her eyes closed, she hadn't seen him yet, a look of such serene relaxation on her face she looked like one of the goddesses themselves, come down to grace the mortal realm with her presence.

She must have sensed his presence or his gaze on her because she opened her eyes and looked right at him. "Laarn!"

A beautiful smile spread over her features, stealing his breath away as she swam toward him. Need and lust raised their heads and roared within him, and in the space between one second and the next, he tore at his clothing, stalking toward her.

His jacket hit the tiles behind him, and he walked out of his boots as he wrenched his pants open, his cock leaping free as he bent to shove them off his hips and down his legs. They were off in seconds, his gaze never leaving hers.

Her cheeks flushed, her eyes darkening as she read the intent on his face, but rather than coming to the steps toward him, she swam backward away from him. His lip curled, a warning growl in the back of his throat, but she just smiled as he waded down the steps into the water.

No words were spoken between them. None were needed. He wanted her, and he was going to have her. The water moved around him as he walked, no, *stalked* her across the pool.

She watched him, the light of mischief in her eyes, a light made brighter the more he growled, acting like the savage warrior he knew humans had dubbed his kind. But his little Jess seemed to like him like this, her cries of pleasure loud when he held her firmly and took what he wanted...what they both wanted.

Before he reached her, she darted to the left, trying to slide past him in the water, but he was ready for her tricks. Throwing himself to the side, it was the work of a couple of powerful kicks and he had his arms around her, hauling her up against his broad chest before she could go under.

She wriggled as if trying to escape, but not too hard. Her delighted gasps were punctuated by the splashes of water around them as he carried her toward the shallower end of the pool. Turning, he sat on one of the inbuilt loungers, the curved tiled "seats" allowing a bather to recline in comfort under the cool water.

It was the work of a moment to set her astride him. She gasped in pleasure as his hard cock slid the length of her pussy lips under the surface, the additives in the water to care for their skin making the ride silky.

Reaching up, he fastened his hand around the nape of her neck, a pang of protectiveness warring with the sheer lust surging through him at how delicate the bones there felt. How delicate she felt. Every time he touched her, he felt like a brute... but he couldn't stop. She was his, his mate... and fire for her burned in his veins.

Pulling her down, he claimed her mouth. Their lips locked and then parted before returning in hot, open-mouthed caresses that drove the need in his body higher. Breaking away for a second, he ran his thumb over her cheek, catching sight of the marks around his wrist. Both Karryl and Tarrick had commed to congratulate him and warn him that if he thought his need for her was slacked now he'd had her, to think again... The lust that burned within for her would only get worse, as would hers for him.

This fact was proved as she wriggled to get closer, taking over their kiss by thrusting her tongue into his mouth in demand. He groaned at the feeling as she teased it along his, rocking her hips to grind her pussy against his thick shaft. That was nothing to the feeling when she slid her hand between them, wrapping her small fingers around his cock and stroking.

"That's it, little human," he broke away to rumble against her lips. "Take it, take what you want from me. It's the Lathar way, and you're mine... so you're Lathar now."

Letting go of her neck, he lay back in the water, spreading his arms in silent invitation. Her gaze shot to his, and then she smiled. The hot look in her eyes had him ready to come then and there. She pumped his cock again, firmer this time, and he groaned as her finger slid over the crown. Every instinct he had urged him to rise up, flip her over and bury himself balls deep in her welcoming softness but he held off. This was for her. For her to take her pleasure from him.

She teased him with her hand, pumping in slow strokes as she reached out with the other. Grabbing his wrist, she brought his hand to her breast in unspoken command. He did as he was bade, cupping and caressing the soft weight of the luscious mound in his hand. She was tiny compared to him, but her breasts more than enough to fill his hands.

He held her, stroking his thumb along the underside before sliding it across the swell of her breast, watching her face as he found her nipple and rubbed it. She bit her lip, eyes closed and head thrown back, a look of erotic concentration on her face. Trying to ignore her siren's touch on his cock, he played with her nipples, stroking and circling, rubbing and tweaking them until they stood out proud, all but begging for his lips and tongue.

Sliding his hand up her back, he urged her to lean forward. A soft swipe of his tongue made her gasp and wriggle, the fingers of the hand on his shoulder turning to claws against his flesh as he teased her anew. Her hand on his cock faltered and she released him for a second to guide the hand he had on her hip between her thighs. Against her breast, his lips curled into a smile at the invite. He didn't need to be asked twice, easing combat-callused fingertips between her slick pussy lips to find her clit.

He stroked and suckled, her body arching and writhing in response to the dual assault. Her hand closed around his cock again, but he kept her too off balance to do more than touch him, or stroke occasionally, ruthlessly driving her up toward need and heat.

"Laarn..." The soft plea of his name on her lips was the sweetest sound he'd heard in his life. "Please..."

"What do you need, little one?" he rasped, sitting up suddenly to claim her lips. "Tell me and I'll give it to you."

"Fuck me," she whispered and he groaned, the words turning him on beyond all belief. "Take me and make me yours again."

He nodded, lying back in the water again. Wrapping both hands around her tiny waist, he lifted her. She helped, repositioning and presenting the head of his cock against her slick entrance. They both groaned as she slid down, impaling herself on his thick cock slowly.

"Ride me, Jess," he groaned, lifting to see where their bodies joined, to where her sweet little pussy stretched wide around his thick cock. Before long, he wouldn't be able to take her like this, she would be too big, her belly swollen with their child. "Ride me as I watch you, looking up in worship of the goddess you are."

"You see me that way? As a goddess?" She looked down at him in surprise, already starting to move.

He gritted his teeth at the erotic slip slide as she lifted up and then impaled herself on him again.

"You're mine. My bond-mate," he managed in a rough voice. "I will always worship you, kneeling at your feet if I must to be granted the boon of touching your beautiful body. I will always crave you, always need you, always want you."

She groaned, the sweetest sound he'd ever heard, and then there were no more words. With each rock of her hips as she rode him, she took them both closer to bliss. He held out for as long as he could, letting her have her way with him, but then she began to falter, her hips losing the rhythm.

Opening her beautiful eyes, she didn't need to say anything. He read the entreaty, the need in them loud and clear. With a growl, he took over, his hands on her hips as he drove up into her. The water lapped and splashed around them as he fucked her with long strokes. Crying out, she collapsed across his chest and he held her, his strength enough for both of them as he moved. Driving up. Stroke after stroke almost turning him inside out with fire as he held off his climax to make it good for her.

Then she whimpered, and her pussy clamped down hard around him as she came, near silently in his arms. He grunted, the spasming of her pussy milking his cock. Fire raced down his spine and around to his balls, his cock jerking as he surged up into her one last time and stiffened. His cock buried inside her to the hilt, he groaned as he emptied his balls into her, jet after jet of hot, ropey seed bathing her inner walls in an explosion of bliss the like of which he'd never experienced before.

Then it was over, and he sagged in the water, glad of its support as he held her close and brushed his lips over her temple. Closing his eyes, he sighed in contentment and happiness.

She was his. Forever.

THE LAST FEW days with Laarn had been amazing.

Jess sighed to herself, lost in happy memories. He was a wonderful lover and insatiable. She wasn't an innocent by any stretch of the imagination, even verged on the adventurous, but she'd had no idea sex could be so... *everything.* So fulfilling. Earth-shattering in its rawness and beauty.

The healer certainly was a dark horse. So stoic and implacable all the time, she'd have never guessed that under that unreadable facade lay a deeply sensual streak that delighted in torturing her with pleasure until she was hoarse screaming his name and boneless with the ecstasy he took her to.

It was more than just the sex, though. There was something else there. A look in his eyes when he touched her, took her... something in there that rocked her right down to her soul.

She couldn't stay away from him either, wanting him again even though he'd come back at lunch. He'd claimed her again... all uncontrolled passion against the door in their quarters, too desperate to even make it to the bed.

And she'd loved it. Every single hot, sweaty, needy second of it.

Loved it and wanted more. Needed more. *Craved* more.

Was that normal for bonded couples? This all-consuming, carnal desperation.

She bit her lip as she made her way through the corridors to the makeshift healer's hall, careful to keep to the smaller halls and corridors so she didn't get caught.

Security had been massively increased in the palace after the purist attack and given the fact she was carrying what could be the savior of the Lathar race, she wasn't supposed to even leave their quarters without the security detail camped in the corridor outside the front door. So she'd slipped out of the garden entrance when they weren't watching.

After all, surprising her husband in his office for a quickie didn't need an audience. She was kinky, but not *that* kinky.

Her heart sped up a little as she reached the large hall they were using while the upper levels of the healer's hall was rebuilt. The south wing of the palace was high ceilinged and flooded with light. Instead of walls, there were simply dividers and screens to create rooms and a big tent of plastic material for the quarantine areas and operating theaters.

Making her way around the edges of the hall on silent feet, she passed the recovery "rooms." Xaandril, badly injured in battle and brought back to the palace by Laarn, was in one of them, Kenna in constant attendance. Jess' lips quirked.

Try as Kenna might to insist her concern for the big general was simply that of one soldier to another, it was obvious to anyone with eyes in their head that something was going on between the two of them. It also hadn't escaped Jess' notice that Xaandril still wore the blue ribbon Kenna had wrapped around his wrist at the tournament.

"I was going to terminate them."

The sound of Laarn's voice stopped Jess just as she reached the area at the back of the hall that had been sectioned off for his lab and office. Her hand fell away from the drape dividing it from the room next door that she'd slipped into. Instinct made her shrink back, out of sight of the semi-translucent panel across the upper third of the drape. Slowly, she edged forward, just enough to peek around the edge.

Two big figures moved about in the area beyond and she easily recognized the other figure as Karryl, Laarn's friend and Jane's mate. The huge warrior was leaning against something on the other side of the office, his arms folded across his chest. He was also right in her line of sight, and she his, so she had to be careful. Any movement and he'd spot her for sure.

"You were?" Karryl asked.

"Yeah." Laarn moved around the bed in the middle of the room. From the metallic sounds and the sparks lighting up around him, he was mending it. She bit her lip again; intelligent, a surgeon and good with tools... was there no end to his talents? "I would have done it as soon as I'd confirmed conception was viable."

Her attention snapped away from the hot image

in her head of Laarn stripped to the waist with a welding torch in his hands and back to the conversation. Conception. He was talking about her pregnancy.

A chill shivered down her spine in warning. She didn't need to be hearing this, shouldn't be listening... but wild horses wouldn't have dragged her away from that spot, her feet rooted to the floor as Laarn continued to speak.

"I never wanted to implant them at all."

"What do you mean? How the *draanth* did she get pregnant then?"

Laarn's chuckle was dry and a little bitter. "Because I'm a fucking idiot and left everything set up in my lab rather than saving the data and terminating the things."

Her heart stuttered in her chest. Things. He was referring to babies, *their babies,* as things.

"But Jess was ill while I was away, and those *draanthing* idiots in the hall made her feel unwelcome, so she used my lab..."

Karryl took up where he left off, realization in his deep tones. "And she used your equipment... the AI completed the implantation sequence."

"You got it in one." Laarn paused and sighed, the outline of his figure moving as he dropped his head, his hand coming up to scoop his hair out of his face. Tears welled in the corners of her eyes as she watched. How many times had she seen that gesture?

"Honestly? I never intended to implant them at all, or claim her. I never wanted that—"

The tears fell, a sob rising in her throat as she backed up, her ears ringing. He didn't want her. He'd never wanted to claim her. Pain lanced through her chest and she stumbled unseen from the hall. Her vision blinded by tears, she somehow made it through the hall and out into the corridors without anyone seeing her.

15

She was in the Imperial gardens. Jess blinked, her eyelashes wet with tears as she looked around. Curled up on one of the benches, she was well out of sight of the main pathways. How long had she been here? It couldn't have been too long. Once her guards had discovered she was gone, all hell would have broken loose. She'd have heard the alarms.

She was glad they hadn't found her though. Not in this state.

A shuddering breath left her as she realized tears still ran down her face silently. She was a fucking idiot. Laarn didn't want her, never had, and he hadn't claimed her until his hand had been forced.

Until *she'd* forced his hand, pushing and pushing

him into a relationship with her. Her cheeks burned with embarrassment. She'd hung around so he couldn't help but notice her, mooned after him like some fucking love-sick teen over her first crush. Then, she let out a bitter laugh, she'd pulled the age-old underhanded female trick and gotten herself pregnant by accident.

Never mind that they hadn't even had sex at that point. Oh no, she'd managed to find a sci-fi equivalent of the immaculate conception. Someone slap her ass and call her fucking Mary. Her hand shook as she shoved it through her hair, the elegant braid she'd put it into this morning long gone under Laarn's hands at lunch.

The memory of their tryst earlier brought fresh tears to her eyes. He fucked her, sure, and he was good at it... so very good... and she'd even thought she'd seen something in his eyes, some sort of emotion. Her snort was bitter. Love. She'd thought it was love, hidden way back there. A love he couldn't admit to yet, hampered by his warrior's training or something. But now she realized differently.

He hadn't wanted to bond with her, so what man wouldn't make the best of a bad job, particularly a man who hadn't had access to a woman for years? No wonder he fucked her with desperation. He was frustrated. Probably had the worst case of blue balls for a fucking century, so when he'd been forced into what amounted to a shotgun wedding...

She closed her eyes and groaned. Oh my god, how fucking stupid was she? No wonder he'd been putting off a bonding ceremony. "After the baby," her ass. He didn't want to be bonded to her at all, and with his knowledge of genetic manipulation... shit, he was probably already looking for a way to remove the bonding marks from his skin.

A wave of exhaustion and nausea washed over her. She'd made a complete and utter fool of herself. Chasing a man who wasn't interested. Had *never* been interested. She'd convinced herself that he was shy or something. He was dedicated to his duty to save the Lathar, but he wasn't shy at all. He never had been.

Casting her mind back, she tried to think of any point when he'd shown interest in her at all. And came up blank. Sure, of all the human women, he'd requested her the most often... she groaned again and let her head rest against the cool marble.

Stockholm Syndrome. She had a classic fucking case of it.

Steps sounded behind her and she jerked upright, grabbing the hem of her skirts to wipe the tears from her eyes. The last thing she wanted to do was admit why she was crying to anyone, to admit her failures and that she'd been a fucking idiot. A small measure of relief filled her as she realized the tread was heavy and male. A Lathar, thank god. She could fool a warrior... fooling one of her friends would have been entirely more difficult. Impossible. After all they'd been through, they could read each other like a book.

Her eyes widened as Saal came into view. A few days had taken care of most of his injuries but he still looked like a man who had been beaten, and badly.

"Shit, Saal..." She looked around in panic. "You have to go. If the guard sees you near me, he'll kill you."

"What I have to say is worth the risk." He managed a small smile as he came nearer and sat on the other end of the bench. His movements were slower than normal and obviously painful. At her little look he shrugged. "None of the healers will touch me past ensuring my life is not in danger, so I have to heal the old-fashioned way. Slowly. To teach me a lesson."

Her heart clenched for him as she took in the bruises on his face, one eye still nearly shut, and across his chest and body. He had to be in agony with the wounds Laarn had inflicted, but to then deny healing as well... a shiver hit her at her mate's ruthlessness.

"I'm sorry," she said softly. "I didn't know accepting help from you would make him do this..."

"No," he interrupted her. "*You* didn't do this. I did. I didn't need to challenge him for you. I didn't need to use you accepting my help as a route to issue that challenge, especially when you did not know our laws. It was a dishonorable move... a, how do you humans say it, a dick move?"

Her lips quirked a little, even through her sadness. "You've been talking to Kenna or Jane," she said, recognizing the comment.

He nodded. "I was reassigned to Lady Jane's protection detail. She's... not you, but is pleasant to be around. I'm hoping that my compliance will stand me in good stead and I might eventually be granted permission to travel to your system. See Earth for myself."

"Yeah?" She smiled, grateful for his understanding and the fact that he hadn't queried the tears on her face or her red, puffy eyes. She shuffled more upright, smoothing her hair down. She must look a right sight. "Are you sure that's because you want to see my planet, or because there are human women—a lot of human women—there?"

He grinned, ducking his head a little and looking up at her through his bangs. "It's the women. You can't blame me, not when I see you and the other ladies here... You're all beautiful and any male would be proud to call you his own."

She shook her head. "Word of warning when you meet more Terran women? Don't go around declaring you own them... we don't like that. It smacks too close to slavery, and we abolished the right to own another human centuries ago."

He blinked, surprise on his face. "You think that's what we mean? That by claiming you, we make you our slaves? *Gods!*"

Shoving a hand into his long hair, he looked at her again. The depth of the shock in his pale eyes would have been amusing if it wasn't so profound.

"You really don't understand our males at all, do you?" he asked. "The dream of all of us is to find a female to claim and call our own. A worthy female who will call the mating marks out of our skin for all to see... but it's not the male who makes a *slave*," he all but spat the word, "of the female, but the other way around. And willingly. Once those marks are on a male's wrist, *he* belongs to *her*. Body, mind and soul. There will never be another female for him as long as he lives. His body, his cock, will never work for another."

Her mouth opened but no words came out, the depth of her surprise was so great. Finally, she cleared her throat and managed, "What. Ever?"

Saal shook his head and then paused and frowned. "Maybe if she died? After years have passed? Usually bonded males whose mates die… well, they're never the same, if you get what I mean? They often go berserk in battle, just keep attacking the enemy until they're exhausted and get killed."

"Oh my…" She really didn't know what to say to that, but was saved from answering as large figures closed in on them suddenly.

Hard hands yanked her off the bench and she screamed, the sound cut off as a hard hand was slapped over her mouth. She carried on screaming, struggling like a wildcat while next to her, Saal bellowed with rage and fought back. But the dark-clad figures around them were too numerous and she watched in horror as they surrounded him. In his injured state, it was obvious any resistance wasn't going to last long.

Her captors lifted her but she twisted and

turned, trying to keep him in sight. She managed it just long enough to see him hit over the back of the head, collapsing to the ground in a heap. Lifeless. She didn't stop screaming and struggling as they carried her away until something sharp was pressed against her neck.

Every cell in her body froze as she stilled, her heart pounding in her chest as a voice rasped in her ear.

"The price for you is dead or alive, Terran bitch. Your call."

"I CAN BLOODY well feed myself, female. Give it here!"

Laarn chuckled at the growl from the general's room as he and Karryl passed, pausing for a moment to get a glimpse into the "room" Xaandril was recovering in and biting back a small smile.

The big warrior was bed-bound, his shoulder and arm bandaged right the way up to the neck with movement suppressors in place, their bright blue lights winking in concert. He couldn't have moved the limb to save his life, just the way Laarn wanted it while his body healed. Sitting next to him on the covers was Kenna, one eyebrow arched as she held out a spoonful of soup.

"And just how are you going to balance the bowl and the spoon without wearing it and burning yourself in the process?" she demanded. "Stop being a big baby and just let me feed you."

Karryl whistled softly, murmuring, "Did she just call the Hero of the Nine Wastes a big baby?"

Laarn chuckled as they passed. "Yes, I do believe she did."

"He's a goner." Karryl fell into step with him as they walked into the main area of the hall. "He just doesn't realize it yet."

"When we took the humans, we assumed they would be docile and biddable like the oonat. Seems the gods played a hell of a joke on us, didn't they? The human women go after what they want, and they don't stop until they get it."

Laarn nodded with a wry smile, stopping by the main station to call up a list of the injuries logged in for treatment. They were the usual assortment of training injuries and one serious burn from engine fuel. Looked like the idiot stuck his arm against a running vent. The healer shook his head at such stupidity. Really, some males should be stopped from breeding.

Karryl's smile was broad as he leaned his hips back against the console next to Laarn, his arms folded over his chest. "Finally realized you were hunted, brother? How do you feel about that? Of all of us, you were the one I never thought would fall..."

"Why not?" Laarn selected one of the open cases for treatment. "I'm a man like any other. A red-blooded male with all the usual drives and needs..." He slid a sideways glance at his friend. "And what makes you think I wasn't the hunter? I had my eye on Jess as soon as I saw her on that base."

And he had. One of the first warriors onto their command deck, he'd noticed her immediately. Kneeling with her hands on the back of her head in the middle of the mass of humans, his gaze had gone directly to her. It didn't matter that there were other females in the room. His attention had been solely for her. She'd been clad in that gods-awful uniform the humans wore, the one that concealed the lines of a woman rather than celebrating them like clothes should.

Then she'd lifted her head, their eyes had met and he'd been sunk.

"*Trallshit,*" Karryl snorted. "You were running scared and everyone knew it."

Caught. Karryl had always been able to see right through him.

"Yeah. But I came to my senses. Thank the gods she managed to get herself with child in my lab before that *draanthic* Saal could make a move on her.

"Speaking of..." Karryl nodded to the other side of the hall. Saal was in the doorway, one hand propping him up. He was covered in blood and unsteady on his feet.

"Huh." Laarn raised an eyebrow. "Wonder who else he pissed off to get another beating?"

Saal staggered forward, his gaze latching onto the two warriors. "The gardens... they took the Lady Jessica," he gasped and then keeled over unconscious on the floor.

BUNDLED into an *oonat* robe with a veil over her face, Jess was taken from the palace and hurried through the streets of the city below. She'd been into the city a couple of times before, but those journeys, in a comfortable carriage surrounded by guards and warriors, bore no relation to being frog-marched through the back streets, only able to get snatched glimpses of where she was through the thick material covering her face.

She tried to remember the twists and turns they took, and how many paces, but before long she was hopelessly lost. Through it all, the hard hand on her arm gripped cruelly, painfully, but thankfully there was no longer a blade at her throat.

But she could hear, and when they hit a crowded area she tried to struggle, opening her mouth to cry out.

Before she could, though, a hard voice said at her ear, "Don't bother. All they see is a handmaiden, a slave. Scream all you like. They wouldn't raise a finger to help you even if we beat you to death right in front of them."

Tears filled her eyes as she realized that he was right. The robes rendered her invisible. The veil was something else, used for handmaidens whose features were presumably too non-Lathar to be palatable. Disgust rose. It was the Lathar equivalent of the human joke about putting a bag on an ugly woman's head so a man could fuck her.

But it meant that he was right. No one would help her, even if she struggled or screamed. She'd seen the scenes themselves. Seen the harsh way some of the Lathar treated their slaves, like they were little more than animals. Not the K'Vass though. She'd never once seen one of their number raise his hand to the robed handmaids. Sure, there was no kindness but there also wasn't cruelty.

They turned a corner and she stumbled on the dusty, hard-packed dirt between two tall buildings. The shadows were chill here and she shuddered in reaction.

"For *draanth's* sake, keep ahold of her," a voice in front of her growled. "She needs to be in good enough shape for the ceremony."

She had to press her lips together hard to suppress her cry of pain as she was hauled upright again and half-carried, half-dragged along. What ceremony? What were they talking about? A bonding ceremony? Fuck that, they'd never get her to agree to bond to anyone, not even if they tortured her.

"Fucking waste if you ask me," the guy holding her growled. "Prime bit of cunt. Why can't they use a beamer to get the brat out, rather than cutting her open? That way we can all have a fuck before we kill her."

Her heart stuttered. Holy shit... They planned to cut her baby out of her? Why? Her question was answered as the man in front of her spoke again.

"Because Dvarr says it's a sacrifice to appease the old gods. They speak to him, have said the bitch's spawn is the goddess made flesh again, and she'll use the Terran women to enslave us."

They were all fucking nuts. Fuck this. Jess started to struggle and scream.

"HELP! I'M TERRAN. THEY'VE KID—"

Pain flared over the back of her head and she staggered, falling to the ground as her vision darkened. Her body went sluggish, no fight in her as she was picked up. There was the sound of booted feet running and then a door crashing open.

"Bitch started yelling but I don't think they followed us."

Dumped unceremoniously on the floor, her veil was yanked off over her head. She was in a house, but not one like the palace.

Instead of smooth marble, this one had sand-colored walls surrounding an interior courtyard. Looking up, she saw the central part of the ceiling was missing, allowing her to see the blue of the sky above, but nothing that would help her.

A fountain gurgled in the middle of the courtyard, water cascading down to the small pool at its base. Sheer panels of floaty fabric fluttered gently in the breeze, their tails brushing the tiled floor gently. All in all, it looked like illustrations of the Roman villas in her automated teaching lessons as a child. She'd always thought they looked so pretty and peaceful—the exact opposite of what she was feeling now as those panels were pushed aside by a warrior as he strode through.

Swallowing her nerves, she scrambled to her feet, stopped from backing up by the two big men behind her. Looking up, her gaze slid over the familiar leathers and parted jacket of a Lathar warrior, and then into the hard, familiar face of the purist leader, Dvarr.

He smiled.

"Welcome to my home, Lady Jessica."

16

"Get me a fucking location *now!*" Laarn growled over the commlink as he stormed through the lower city streets, a blade in one hand and a pulse pistol in the other. He knew he presented a formidable sight in full battle armor, his hair flying around his shoulders as he kicked doors down and stormed through houses.

Maids scattered as he entered the next house, the high-pitched shriek of terrified *oonat* getting on his nerves as he ripped through rooms but found them empty of his prey.

"*FUCK!*" He turned in a circle in the shady interior courtyard, fists white-knuckled around his weapons.

They'd stolen Jess right out from under his nose.

From the palace gardens no less. He still couldn't understand why she'd even been there on her own, and he'd raged at her guards. Demanding to know how the *fuck* they'd let her out of their sight when they knew what was at stake. When they knew the entire fate of their race rested on the shoulders of one delicate little Terran female and the child she carried.

No.

He stopped dead, a frown creasing his brow. The drapes whispered around him in the breeze that lifted strands of his hair across his face. The rage inside him, the panic... it had nothing to do with losing the last piece of the puzzle to save his species. Even if Jess had been just a normal woman, nothing remarkable about her DNA or the child she carried, he would *still* be incensed... furious... terrified and desperate to find her.

Because she was his, the baby was his and he loved them both.

He blinked, every cell in his body motionless as the knowledge resounded through him.

He loved her.

He loved Jessica with every fiber of his being.

Closing his eyes, he let his head drop back as he let out a groan of despair.

He loved her and he might have lost her forever.

Fear gripped his heart as he pushed himself into motion again, storming from the house. New purpose filled him. If he had to search every fucking dwelling in the city to find her, he would. Someone, somewhere, knew where she'd been taken and by whom. When he found out, he was going to tear their spines from their bodies with his bare hands.

And *when* he found her—when, not if—he growled under his breath, "I am *so* chaining you to that fucking bed."

"Somehow, I don't think that was for me." Karryl grinned as he appeared at Laarn's side, fully armed and armored the same as the slender figure behind him. Laarn lifted an eyebrow, recognizing Karryl's mate, the human soldier, Jane.

"Don't ask." Karryl growled as he spotted the direction of Laarn's gaze. "You know human women. They do what they want, when they want. At least if she fights with me, I can keep an eye on her."

"True." Laarn's gaze flicked down to the blood across Karryl's neck and the eyebrow went up again. "Yours?"

"No." The warrior shook his head, his braids dancing and the valor beads catching the light. Soon it was likely both he and Laarn would have to cut their hair: Laarn to take up the role of lord healer and, if the rumors he'd heard were true, Karryl to become a war commander with his own group of ships.

"We ran into a mouthy one. Sympathizer. He's had an attitude readjustment."

"Readjustment?"

Karryl chuckled. "He made a crude comment about human women where Jane could hear him. She educated him on the error of his ways." Suddenly the warrior frowned, touching the comm in his ear. "Someone two blocks over saw a couple of warriors dragging a veiled female through the back alleys a while back. Want to bet that's our girl?"

"*My* girl," Laarn growled possessively. Even though he knew Karryl was mated and equally possessive over the woman at his side, he didn't like any other male laying claim to Jess, even verbally.

"*Your* girl, got it." Karryl held his hands up in surrender as he and Jane turned to go. Laarn couldn't help noticing that already they moved as a unit, Karryl watching the rear as his slender mate took point. The big warrior cast him a glance. "You coming or not?"

By the time they got two blocks over, the emperor and reinforcements had arrived, warriors crowding into a back alley that had been cleared of merchants and furniture from the street cafes. Laundry from the neighboring houses fluttered in the breeze overhead, shielding them from the baking sun.

Daaynal was grim-faced as he flung a bruised and battered warrior into the dirt at Laarn's feet. Blood streaked one side of his face and his left arm hung limply, the upper arm at a funny angle. The healer in Laarn, though, was well and truly dormant as he looked down at the male. It was one of the guards from Jess' security detail.

"This fucking *draanthic* sold us out. He's one of Dvarr's. We caught him trying to steal out of the palace on the sly."

"Shit," Jane breathed, pulling off her helmet to look down on the fallen male with disgust. She looked up and met Laarn's gaze, looking between him and Daaynal. "It all makes sense now. I couldn't figure out how she'd slipped past a group of battle-hardened warriors like that. I mean, me or Kenna?" She shrugged. "Yeah, you boys haven't a hope in hell of stopping us if we want out..."

A warrior behind Daaynal snorted. "Really? A woman? Our warriors would easily catch you and restrain you."

A chill descended as Jane looked the young warrior right in the eye. Laarn almost felt sorry for him as her voice, cold as space, sliced through the silence.

"Really? Perhaps you should have been on hand to offer your wisdom to Ishaan F'Naar or maybe the T'Laat then. I'm sure Ishaan in particular would have benefited," she said, naming the clan leader she'd shot point-blank between the eyes and the clan who thought it would be a good idea to try and kidnap the human women from the K'Vass.

The warrior wisely shut up, backing up a step under Jane's steely gaze. She returned her attention to Laarn and Daaynal. "Jess was Ops, so the idea that she could slip past your detail didn't sit right with me."

"Ops?" Laarn asked with a frown.

"Base operations... traffic I think. Basic military training but not combat personnel," she explained. "We wouldn't put her on a battlefield. She's too valuable doing her primary role."

Karryl advanced on the bloodied warrior, a snarl of anger on his face. "So this asshole let her go..."

"...And told his buddies where to find her," Daaynal finished the sentence for him, reaching the male before Karryl and hauling him to his feet with a hard hand on the back of his neck. Trapped between the two bigger warriors, he went pale, and started to talk... words falling from his lips in a panicked stream.

"It was Dvarr... he threatened us all," he stammered. "Threatened to wipe out our entire clan if we didn't find some way to get the girl to him. When she wandered off by herself—" He squawked as Daaynal's hand tightened. "He's in there. They were going to perform the ceremony at sunset."

Laarn's eyes narrowed. "What fucking ceremony?"

Silence fell in the small group as they waited for the answer, all eyes trained on the pale, panicked male.

"A...a sacrifice to appease the gods. If the Terran and her spawn die, the gods will favor us."

Fear that he might be too late tried to take hold but a glance at the skyline assured him that sunset was still a way off. It was traditional to offer sacrifices as the sun went down and Dvarr was a traditionalist... so surely he wouldn't do anything before sunset in case that displeased the gods. But... He was also a fucking lunatic. Who knew *what* he was thinking?

Laarn roared, rage and panic filling him, but

before he could land a blow on the sniveling creature, Daaynal wrapped a big arm around his neck and wrenched. The loud crack of bone snapping filled the alleyway before the warrior dropped, lifeless, to the ground, his neck snapped and his eyes wide and unseeing.

"To live without honor is no life at all," Daaynal snarled. "So he will not live. Apparently Dvarr is holed up in there—" He nodded to the bigger house at the end of the street opposite them. "What say we go and crash this fucking ceremony they have planned?"

Laarn was already moving, intent on marching down the street and kicking the door in to rescue his mate. Rage surged through him, white hot and volatile, ready to explode at any moment. They had his woman, and his child, and they planned to kill them.

Daaynal stopped him with a large hand in the middle of his chest and nodded toward the roofline. In his rage Laarn had missed the squat outline of automated defenses half hidden in the tiles.

"Don't be a hero, son," the big emperor murmured. "At least until your female can see and coo appropriately."

Laarn snarled, about to knock his uncle's hand

away when a new sound registered. The *thump-thump-thump* of bot feet. *Heavy* bot feet. As he watched, a troop of *drakeen* combat bots rounded the corner and took up position in front of them, slowly moving forward toward their target.

"Nice to see the big guns here," Karryl whistled, falling into place beside Laarn and Daaynal as they followed the bots, using the cover they afforded.

True to form, before they'd gotten halfway up the street, the automated defenses on the roof of Dvarr's villa activated. The cover plates lifted, twin snub-nosed canons edging into view. Instantly they locked onto the group and the next moment the air was filled with laser blasts.

The bots moved, their mechanical arms a dance of metal and energy fields as they caught the incoming fire, protecting the men, and one woman, behind them. Laarn shot his uncle a sideways look. The destroyer-bots of the Lathar armory, *drakeen* were rarely deployed in groups of more than two, yet there were five in front of them and at least three bore the personal insignia of the emperor. Which begged the question, where the hell had Daaynal found so many pilots. *Drakeen* were hellishly difficult to pilot, and not many had the aptitude for it...

Then he spotted the uplink band around the back of Daaynal's head, half hidden under his hair and snug to the scalp, and blinked in surprise, looking at the three bots with the emperor's mark again. Sure enough, all three moved easily, but with a strange synchronicity that the other two didn't.

"All three are yours?" he asked, catching his uncle's eye as he rechecked his primary assault weapon automatically.

The corner of Daaynal's lips quirked up as he did the same, sliding the weapon back into the sheath at his thigh. Two more pistols were in bandoliers across his wide chest. None of his movements betrayed the fact he was also piloting three heavy bots when most couldn't pilot one without lying down in a dark room.

"Your mother rewrote the code for them when we were kids," he murmured with a wink. "Don't tell anyone... it'll be our little secret."

Shit... Laarn blinked again, rolling his shoulders as they neared the villa. No wonder no one had ever challenged Daaynal for the throne, not when he had tricks like that up his sleeve.

Then there was no more time to think about anything other than getting his female and baby out of Dvarr's clutches.

"The plan?" he demanded as the bots formed into a line, bringing their guns to bear on the front doors of the villa.

Daaynal grinned, unsheathing both his sword and rifle. "Kick the doors down, kill the bastards inside and rescue your woman. What else?"

Laarn grinned, weapons in his hands as the canons on the bots whined when they powered up.

"My kind of plan."

They were going to kill her.

Jess bit back her whimper, not wanting to give the men who held her, her arms twisted painfully behind her back, the satisfaction. Dropping her head, she let her hair cover her face and squeezed her eyes shut tightly.

She'd been dragged into the main hall of the villa a few minutes ago to find it packed with warriors. The furniture had been cleared to the side to make room for them all to stand in lines, like they were in church. Forced to her knees on the hard stone floor in front of them, Dvarr stood a few feet away, chanting.

She winced as she moved, trying to clear the

rubble and dirt digging into her knees. Lifting her head, she looked around. The floor hadn't been swept, and the cobwebs gathering in the corners of the room said the villa had been unlived in for a while. Which meant no owners to come home and find a bunch of fanatics had taken it over.

Dust motes danced in the air as Dvarr spoke, twirling in the shafts of sunlight from the vents above them. For a moment she allowed herself to get lost in their simple dance, stretching out the moment of just being alive as long as she could and pushing back thoughts of the horrors she knew were to come.

His voice rose and fell hypnotically. It was a language she vaguely recognized as Latharian, but couldn't make out properly. Like it was an older version of something similar. Perhaps there were other languages on their planet—like French, English and others on Earth... It was beautiful, even if it did fill her with dread.

Whatever he was saying, his audience were rapt, their eyes trained on him fanatically. She shivered at the looks on their faces as panic and fear welled up.

Dvarr was going to kill her. Worse, he was going to cut the baby right out of her body. Her gaze focused on the knife in his hands. Curved and serrated on the back, its wickedly sharp inner blade glinted in the dim light.

A whimper broke from her lips and she struggled again, but it was no good. The two men at her side held her easily, their hands biting cruelly into her arms and shoulders. They were so close she could smell their sweat and the sickly-sweet odor of whatever they'd used to draw a red line down one side of their faces. The same red line as all the Lathar in the room had... a sign of their cult or whatever they called their group.

Tears formed at the backs of her eyes, welling up to stream down her cheeks in scalding rivers. There was no way out. It wasn't fair. Always in books or films there was something clever the heroine could do to extricate herself from a tricky situation, or the hero charged in at the last moment to save the day.

This was real life, though, not a story. No one knew where she was and it was becoming painfully apparent that real life didn't give a shit about her expectations and what was fair. The universe was a cruel and unforgiving thing... there would be no happily ever after for her and her baby. No crib in the beautiful room next to their bedroom in the palace. No seeing Laarn hold their daughter for the first time. More tears ran down her face as her heart twisted savagely in her chest... she'd never see if she had her father's eyes.

Dvarr turned to her guards. "Get her up here."

She was yanked to her feet, kicking and screaming as she was hauled in front of the fanatic leader. One of the guards growled, quelling her fight by pulling an arm back and punching her in the jaw. Her head snapped around, agony and blackness welling up as blood filled her mouth. She managed to spit it out, woozy as Dvarr made her stand in front of him, tsking under his breath as he had to support her with an arm around her ribs just under her bust.

He continued chanting, the sound making her head swim. She watched in horrified fascination as he lifted the blade. It hung in the air above her, the edge caught in one of the shards of sunlight piercing the shadows of the room.

It plunged downward. Tore into her stomach.

She gasped, looking down. Blood welled around the blade, turning her skirts scarlet. Eyes wide, she watched helpless as Dvarr's hand tightened around the hilt, seesawing the blade through her flesh, and she realized the terrible screaming in her ear was coming from her own throat.

The sound of pain and suffering was only drowned out when the doors exploded inward, killing three warriors instantly, and the gap was filled with warriors.

It was too late.

She smiled as her gaze met Laarn's horrified one, the angle shifting as Dvarr dropped her to the ground and raced forward to face the intruders, willing him to understand it was okay.

Then her eyes fluttered shut and she couldn't open them again.

17

"*No!*" Laarn saw Jess fall and his heart felt like it had been torn clean from his chest to tumble to the floor next to her. A feral, wounded bellow escaped him, ripping its way up from the depths of his soul to give voice to his pain. Launching himself into movement, he tore into the warriors in front of him, carving a path with blade and assault pistol.

No one who stood before him survived. Red-striped faces fell and were instantly forgotten as he fought his way toward the crumpled figure on the other side of the room. The war cries of his fellow warriors sounded behind him but he paid them no mind, his entire focus on reaching Jess. Everything passed in a blur, so fast, yet it felt like an eternity until he reached her, falling to his knees by her fallen form. His weapons clattered discarded to the dusty floor, no use to him now.

"Gods, Jess... can you hear me?"

For a moment, he was frozen, paralyzed into place as his hands, usually so sure, hovered above her crumpled body. She lay on her back, her hair spread around her head like a dark halo, the horrific wound in her abdomen staining her dress and the floor around her bright scarlet. She was so pale and still that his heart stuttered, all his senses telling him that he'd lost her.

Then her eyes fluttered open and his healer's instincts kicked him in the ass. Shoving his hand down over her stomach to apply pressure, he bellowed over his shoulder for his healer's pack and a stretcher.

"You're going to be okay, Jess. I promise," he told her, groveling in the dirt next to her to smooth the hair back from her face. "Just stay with me, love, please." He was begging where everyone could see him, the proud lord healer brought low, but he didn't care. He'd give anything to save her, including his rank, title... even his life.

She blinked at him, her eyes unfocused and he

thought she was slipping again, his heart giving a savage lurch. Then her small hand crept over his.

"Save her…" she whispered, her voice weak. "You didn't… want me… or her. But save her, please…"

Her eyelids fluttered down and he panicked, grabbing with one hand at the pack someone dropped down next to him.

"What? No… Jess, stay with me." Tearing the pack open, he reached for pressure-sprays one-handed, snapping them open and pressing them into her flesh around the tear in her stomach.

His keen eyes studied the site of the wound, watching as the pressure sprays took effect and slowed the bleeding down, but it was only a patch. It wouldn't hold long. *Shit.* Where was the damn stasis stretcher? It was taking too long. Before he could open his mouth to yell, though, he heard Daaynal's deep voice shouting at people to move out of the way.

"Stay awake, love," he urged Jess. "Tell me what you mean. I've always wanted you."

Her eyes took longer to open this time, and her voice was so weak that he had to lean forward to hear her. "Heard you… Karryl… You were going… terminate. Didn't want to be bond—" Her words cut off as her head fell to the side, her delicate frame too weak to keep her conscious, but he heard her and her words sliced him right down to the soul.

She thought he didn't want her. Had used her last strength to beg him to save their baby, no thought for her own life. In that moment Laarn was truly humbled, his little mate displaying a strength that had nothing to do with speed or muscle or combat ability. Standing back, he kept a sharp eye on the stasis team as they loaded her gently into the stretcher and activated it. He only let himself breathe a small sigh of relief when the unit was active and he could see her vitals level out.

The fight was done, but he didn't even spare a glance for Dvarr and his men, either those that had been captured or those who lay dead on the floor around them. Walking by the stretcher, he paused for a moment when Daaynal caught his attention.

"How bad?" The emperor didn't mince words, his hand on Laarn's arm and his expression concerned.

"Bad." Laarn didn't bother to hide the distraught note in his voice. "I need to operate. Now."

Daaynal dropped his hand, nodding. "Go. We'll sort this."

Laarn paused for a moment, his gaze sliding to the prisoners. Dvarr was on his knees, force restraints around his ankles, wrists and neck. Hatred surged, hard and fast, almost cutting off Laarn's breathing.

"Him. Make sure he's still alive when I'm done," he snarled. "I want to fucking gut him myself."

With that he turned and followed the stasis stretcher out of the ruined building. Before he could exact revenge, he had to save his woman.

They were rushed back to the palace with a *drakeen* bot escort. The big machines surrounded them, making sure people on the streets moved out of the way. Laarn had the impression of curious faces, then sorrow and anger as those in the crowd realized that one of the human women had been badly hurt.

"Gods guide you, Lord Healer."
"Gods bless the Terran lady."
"May the gods save her."

Voices called out blessings and well-wishes as they passed, and Laarn managed a smile or two in thanks. It was reassuring that most of the Lathar weren't of the same mind as Dvarr and his asshole followers. Most of them seemed genuinely upset and worried about Jess' health. He made a mental note to pass that onto Daaynal later but then realized he didn't have to. Two of the bots surrounding them had Imperial marks, so what they saw, the emperor saw.

Tovan waited for them at the entrance to the healer's hall, his arms folded and his expression forbidding. As soon as he saw them, he hurried forward, peering into the stasis stretcher. At the sight of Jess lying there, motionless and covered in blood, he paled, visibly shaken as he looked up at Laarn. "We heard on the comms but I didn't think... he tried to..."

Laarn's voice was hard as he motioned the stretcher in ahead of them, all his emotions locked down. "Dvarr tried to cut the baby from her womb. I've applied pressure patches but we need to work fast or we'll lose them both."

"That *animal*," Tovan hissed, his expression furious. "Never in my life have I been ashamed to call myself Lathar, but I am now. How could any male worthy of the name hurt such a lovely creature as Lady Jessica?"

Laarn looked at him, noting his expression and the faces of the healers behind him. They were furious and he knew in that moment that no purist out there would ever receive treatment from an Imperial healer ever again. Tovan took a shuddering breath and looked at him directly. "The main theater has been prepared for you, my lord. Please, come this way..."

When they walked into the main area, sweeping through the drapes in a rustle of plastic, Laarn was surprised to find not the usual one, but three operating units set up.

"We won't let you take this one alone, my lord," Tovan said quietly. "You've been in battle and the lady is badly injured. We'll be standing by in case you need us to take over. Between us all, we can save her."

Laarn inclined his head. Tovan had been one of the most outspoken of the healers against the possibility the Terran women could be the saviors of their race, so to go from that to being willing to take on Jess' pain and save her... it would have warmed him through had he been thinking right.

"Support only, monitor her vitals and inform me if any other issues crop up. Do not initiate the link unless the worst happens," he ordered, knowing damn well the only way he'd hand over responsibility for Jess' healing was if he no longer drew breath. "She is my woman and my responsibility."

The other healers nodded, stepping out of the way as he stripped off his armor and leather jacket, letting them drop unheeded to the floor. Stepping through the decontamination unit, he kept his eyes locked on Jess as he approached the uplink unit. Arms out, he just nodded as Tovan and his assistant slid the gauntlets over his hands and wrists, locking them into place.

"Neural interface ready, surgical unit online," Tovan said, looking over. "Ready when you are, my lord."

"Do it." Laarn's voice was clipped and firm. "Take me in now."

"Aye, my lord. I'll ease you in—"

"*No!*" Laarn barked. "She's in pain, a *lot* of pain. Give it to me, all of it."

He heard the hiss as Tovan prepared to argue but then silence. Protocol was to ease into the uplink, giving the healer time to prepare to take the pain load, but they didn't have time for that. Just one look at Jess' vitals said she was in trouble and he needed to work fast.

"Transferring."

Laarn grunted as pain exploded through him, all centered in his lower stomach. It was a cutting, biting agony that stole his breath and nearly his reason. The wound was... would have been mortal.

He could feel the very wrongness of it. It should have killed her but somehow hadn't.

Straightening, he activated the unit, his keen eyes already spotting where he would need to be working. The blade had dug deep, curling around her womb and nicking it, but not cutting into the amniotic sac. The baby was okay... would be okay... *if* he could save her mother.

"Heart rate increasing..."

Tovan's voice sounded in the background, a constant update on the readouts Laarn wasn't paying attention to at the moment as he started to work on the terrible wound in Jess' stomach. He worked fast, sweat pouring from him as he fought his own fear and feelings to maintain the link with her. To take her pain away even as he worked to repair the damage to her body. He created new molecular strings, binding them together to mend the rent flesh. He stitched cells, mended veins and arteries but try as he might, as soon as he mended one area, another failed.

"Shitshitshit..." He began to panic. He couldn't do this. Couldn't maintain the neutral focus he needed to operate when it was the woman he loved on the table. His grandfather had been right. He couldn't be lord healer and love as well.

"Blood pressure dropping. We're losing her!"

Tovan's voice was sharp and almost at the same moment, Laarn felt a new presence alongside him, brushing his mind with reassurance.

"Who's uplinked?" he demanded, his voice sharp with anger. He'd told them all to stay out. His grip on this was tenuous enough. He couldn't have someone else in here fucking it all up further.

"No one! There's no one else in there with you, I swear," Tovan replied, confusion in his tone.

Laarn blinked, his hands still as he analyzed the new presence. He'd uplinked with others before, usually for training, but he'd never felt a healer this strong. Never. He blinked as the new healer added their strength to his, allowing him to take the lead in a quiet, understated way. He breathed a sigh of relief as some of the pain load reduced and he could focus.

Starting work again, he kept his focus on repairing the terrible wounds but also studied the new presence alongside him. As his hands moved, part of his mind was detached from what he was doing, working through the puzzle. Whoever it was, they were easily as strong as he was. Tovan swore no one had uplinked through the other units, and a quick query proved that was true. And he'd never heard of anyone being able to remote uplink to a surgical unit. Ever. Yes, it was possible for the bots, but not surgery. So that meant whoever it was, was in the room and not uplinked. Which narrowed down the candidates to just the two people in... the... link.

It couldn't be Jess, the healer read as Lathar... Laarn blinked, his hands stilling for a moment as he focused on the other presence. A healer he'd never met, one as powerful as he was himself, maybe even more so... He sent an incredulous query and was met with a burst of pleasure, love, and a greeting.

His daughter.

Tears rolled down his face. Somehow, impossibly, his daughter was already aware and just as determined to save her mother as he was. With the added strength, his hands moved faster, faster than he'd ever thought possible. Where before he'd been mending at the molecular level, he went deeper, at the nano-molecular and beyond, checking the atomic layer. He'd never been this deep before, and curiosity spurred him forward until a small chide from his daughter's presence wrapped around his and pulled him back.

Full of wonder, he returned to his task, the sense of urgency gone now. He could *see* at a glance what he needed to do to save Jess' life... the life of the woman he loved. She was everything, his life, his love... his very reason for being, and he loved her. He'd thought he couldn't have both, love and be lord healer... his grandfather's words that love weakened a healer had always haunted him, but as he worked he realized something.

His grandfather had been wrong.

Love, his love for Jessica, the love he had and felt returned from his daughter, it was *everything*. Denying his feelings had only hampered him as a healer. Denied him his true power. So he let go of his mental blocks, the fetters he'd trained to put on his emotions. Instantly, a jolt of power flowed through him, surprised voices from the healers in the room heard but not listened to as he surged into motion. Repairing. Rebuilding. Healing.

Finally, he was done, removing the last traces of the scar across his little Terran's abdomen with a smile. His body ached with remembered pain and tension racked his broad shoulders but he didn't care. He'd done it. He'd saved his mate's life.

They'd saved her.

With a burst of gratitude and love directed at his daughter, he wrapped his mental presence around hers for a long moment in the nearest he could get to a hug. Warmth filled him in return and for a moment, he saw her in his mind's eye—tall and slender, with his eyes and Jess' dark curls, she was stunningly beautiful. And… he realized, his gaze dropping to her scarred arms… a healer like him. With a curve of her lips, the image disappeared and he dropped out of the link, convinced he'd just had a glimpse of the future.

He opened his eyes as Tovan unclipped the gauntlets, wonder in his eyes and a smile on his face. "Your mate is resting peacefully, and her prognosis is good. My lord… you did it. Well done."

Laarn smiled, his gaze flitting over the sleeping woman. Her color was good, and all she needed now was rest. As did he.

"Thank you, my friend. Wake me in a couple of hours."

With that, he made his way to organize a cot so he could sleep next to her.

18

He looked worn out.

Jess lay on her side, watching Laarn sleep on the cot next to her bed. She'd woken a while back, warm and comfortable, surprised to find herself in the healer's hall and, it appeared when she investigated her stomach, healed. There was no wound, or even any dressing, to mark where Dvarr had plunged a knife into her stomach. Panic had assaulted her, her first thought for the baby she carried, but within a few seconds a sense of warmth and calm had washed over her and the worry had receded. Try as she might, she couldn't bring it back. Everything would be okay. The baby was fine... Laarn would have seen to it.

He really was handsome. Her gaze wandered

over him. He lay on his back on the cot, his wide shoulders filling the narrow space. He'd left off his jacket, so all his scars were on display, but they didn't bother her. Instead, she traced each and every one with her gaze. They were proof her man was amazingly strong.

"I always worried that they'd bother you."

His deep voice was low and rough. She blinked and looked up. He hadn't moved at all, but his eyes were open, watching her intently without a hint of sleepiness in his gaze.

"Why would you think that?" She kept her voice low to match his. Intimate. Secrets shared just between the two of them.

He shrugged one big shoulder slightly. "I read your medical texts. Humans remove scars whenever possible. Jane corroborated that as well, said it's common and your species also alters their appearance with cosmetic surgery. These..." he paused, and indicated his body. "I'll never get rid of them. I will always have them."

She frowned, shook her head as he levered himself up to a sitting position. His hair, unbound, fell around his shoulders as he rested his elbows on his knees to look at her. There were lines of strain around his eyes and he still looked tired.

"I don't want you to get rid of them. They're who you are. And, despite the fact that some of my species are all-consumed by appearance, I'm not one of them."

She moved to sit up and he was there instantly, strong arms wrapped around her to help her.

"Easy there, you just had major surgery. You might be a little sore," he warned, settling her back against the pillows. She refused to let him go, wrapping her hands around his heavily-muscled upper arms and looking up into his face.

"The baby?"

A smile curved his lips. "Our daughter is fine. Healthy."

"Oh, thank god." Relief made her feel weak and she leaned her forehead against his shoulder, savoring the embrace. "I was so scared, Laarn. I couldn't do anything to stop him killing her... me... We would have been dead if you hadn't rescued us."

He'd come to her rescue... and she had to let him go. Her relief faded away, replaced by misery. She loved him but she had to let him go, had to let him live the life he would have had before she'd forced decisions upon him.

Gathering herself, she looked up, into the green eyes she loved so much.

"Thank you for saving me too... I didn't expect you to. I just wanted you to save her." Drawing a shaking breath, she let him go. Every cell in her body cried out at the loss but she steeled herself against it. Her baby was alive. That's all she needed to know. All she could... *would*... ask. "But I'd like you to leave now, please."

"What?" Sharpness entered his voice as he stood in front of her. "Leave? You're my mate... *and* in case it escaped your notice, I'm also your healer. I'm not going anywhere. Jess? Jess... look at me. Has this got something to do with what you said before? That I didn't want you?"

"I heard you talking." She managed to get the words out but refused to look up, mangling the sheets over her lap in her hands. "Heard you tell Karryl that you'd never intended to implant... to get me pregnant. That you never wanted to claim me."

Taking a shuddering breath, she looked up, knowing tears welled in her eyes but not able to do a damn thing about it. "So I release you from the claim. I'll divorce you, or whatever the hell the Lathar call it... I'll let you go to live your life."

He looked down at her, his face unreadable, apart from the small muscle in the corner of his jaw that pulsed. "We have no divorce." His voice was hard, pulsing with anger. "You can't release me from the claim."

"But why?" It was a plea, pure and simple. "I thought you'd be happy about it."

He moved, faster than she'd expected, and gathered her into his arms, drawing her into his lap on the bed. She gasped as his lips claimed hers, determined that she wouldn't respond. That lasted all of three seconds before she whimpered and kissed him back, her emotions overwhelmed. She hadn't thought she'd get the chance to kiss him again, either through her own death, or letting him go. Whatever, being in his arms again hadn't seemed at all likely so she had no defenses against him.

When he lifted his head, she was breathless... looking up at him silently.

"You're not releasing me. *I'm* not releasing you," he growled, strong fingers under her chin. "For the simple fact I love you, and I'm fairly sure you love me too."

She blinked, eyes wide. "You... what?"

"I love you. And I'll keep kissing you until you believe it." He leaned down to kiss her again, this time his lips lingering for long moments.

"You only heard *half* the conversation with Karryl. If you'd stayed to listen to the rest, you'd have heard me tell him that no, I didn't want to claim you... but I'm so fucking glad you did the claiming. You'd have heard me tell him that I didn't want to implant those pregnancies, because I wanted to get you pregnant the old-fashioned way... but that I'm not sorry that you are."

He tucked the loose strands of her hair behind her ear gently. "Jessica Kallson, I've loved you since I saw you kneeling on the floor when we captured your base. Why do you think I kept pulling you in for tests? I didn't need them. I just wanted to see you, and I was too much of an idiot to realize it. I thought..."

He dropped his head back for a moment and closed his eyes.

"This is going to sound so fucking stupid. As healers we're always told that we can't have emotions, that we can't feel because it interferes with our ability to heal. I didn't think I could take a mate and still be a healer. Still be the lord healer the empire needs."

Her hopeful mood, the seed that had been growing in the center of her chest, stalled. "I-I wouldn't want to stop you doing your job..."

"You won't." He dropped his head and speared her with his gaze. "When Dvarr took you, I was terrified I'd lost you... when I saw you fall..." His expression became haunted.

"Nothing mattered anymore. All my life it's been about duty, about becoming strong enough, skilled enough, to become lord healer... about saving the Lathar. But when you fell, when I thought I'd lost you—" He broke off and shuddered. "I didn't care about any of it. Without you, there is nothing. No meaning. No reason for any of it."

The raw emotion in his eyes, in his voice, brought tears to her eyes. She couldn't look away, reaching up to touch his face, smooth her fingertips over his jaw. Opening her mouth to speak, she didn't manage a word before he cut her off.

"No, please... let me get this out." He settled her more comfortably against him. "I had always been told emotions were anathema to a healer. That we should remain dispassionate and neutral. But when *you* were there on the table, someone taught me that emotions are the most powerful weapon I have as a healer. Taught me to *use* them. I wouldn't have been able to save you without her or that lesson."

He slid his hand into her hair and tilted her head up for another kiss. "I love you, Jess. Now, please, put me out of my misery and tell me I haven't lost any chance of you loving me back."

He loved her. He really loved her. Tears in her eyes, she shook her head. "I've always loved you, from the moment I saw you, I think. I just couldn't bear to think that I'd forced you into a shotgun wedding, or that you were only with me because of the baby."

"A shotgun wedding?" He frowned, a puzzled smile on his lips. "Does that mean I have to kidnap you from your family armed to the teeth to make you mine? I'll do it, if you need me to. Whatever you need, whenever you need... I'm yours, Jess. I love you. Be mine?"

"Yes... *yes!*" Throwing her arms around his neck, she hugged him tightly, burying her face against his neck. She never wanted to let him go.

"I love you," she mumbled into his hair, her eyes closed in sheer and utter relief. "Please, don't ever leave me again."

"Love," he rumbled by her ear. "I don't intend to let you out of my sight ever again. The last time I went off planet you managed to get yourself pregnant. The next time, I plan on getting you with child myself."

She laughed, pulling back to look at him. His green eyes were alight with love and amusement.

Reaching up, she kissed him again. It was a long, slow kiss, delicate and sensual but full of promise and love. Finally, she broke away to look at him and frowned.

"She?"

He blinked, confusion on his face. "What?"

"You said she... that she taught you to use your emotions? Who was she?"

She ran through the names of the human women on the planet in her mind, wondering who it was that had that level of wisdom and awareness so she could thank them. But Laarn just smiled and moved to place a big hand on her stomach.

"Our daughter."

Deep within, almost as though she could feel her father's hand, there was the tiniest flutter. Jess gasped and looked into his eyes for confirmation. He nodded, spreading his fingers wide as if to protect them both.

"She's aware of us both, and powerful. A more powerful healer than I am for sure. She helped me see that I needed to use my love for you to save you, and she helped me do it. You're mine, Jessica Kallson, both of you. And I'll love you both as long as I live. On that, you have my word as lord healer, a warrior..."

He dipped his head again and brushed his lips over hers.

"...And the man who loves you."

***

Ready for the next Warriors of the Lathar story?

Thank you for taking a chance on **Pregnant by the Alien Healer.** I hope you enjoyed it!

If you did, it would be great if you could leave a **review** - even if it's just a little one. Every review makes a huge difference to an author and helps other readers find and enjoy the book as well!

I'm happy to say that the next book in the Lathar series, **Alien Healer's Baby** is ready and waiting for you! (Turn the page for a preview of the cover if it doesn't show!)

P.S. If you're new to me and my books, or haven't had chance to check it out yet, go take a look at my **Kyn Warriors** Series. Like the Lathar, but vampires instead!!

P.P.S. Sign up to my VIP mailing list and I'll shoot you a quick notification when my new books releases: **http://mina-carter.com/newsletter/**

READ AN EXCERPT FROM ALIEN COMMANDER'S MATE...

WARRIORS OF THE LATHAR BOOK 6

*F*enriis had never heard the sound of a woman's tears. It was both the most beautiful thing he'd ever heard and the most terrible. It sounded like her heart was breaking.

He hadn't intended to reveal himself. His plan had been to drop in, check that the Kallson woman was alive, unharmed and being cared for by someone. So when he'd heard voices he'd concealed himself quickly. Not sure if he'd meet with resistance, he'd chosen to wear body armor just in case. A sound move since his armor's refractive camouflage and the shadows of the ruined building had allowed the two humans to walk right past him.

But he hadn't seen them. He'd been turned away

from the door in the room he'd been in and although the camouflage was good, it wasn't perfect. Human eyes were like those of the Lathar... those of an apex predator, drawn to movement. He'd remained stock-still, unable to see but able to hear everything that occurred between the humans.

A man and a woman... a couple, he'd realized quickly when the male had asked the female to become his wife. His mate, he quickly translated from human to Lathar. Then he winced at the female's reaction. Yeah, he wasn't the best with females, given the Lathar no longer had any, but even he knew... *draanth,* any male of any species with anything approaching common sense would have realized... that proposing to a female with anything of a previous partner's was a bad idea. Like *really* bad. Apocalyptically bad.

He'd thought the female was about to eviscerate the male at that point, using just the iciness of her voice. He'd kept his chuckle to himself at the male's clueless response. Human males were *dense.* The realization made him feel a little less guilty about stealing their women away. The *draanthic* didn't deserve them anyway. Latharian males made far better mates.

The male had stormed off in a huff, leaving the

female alone in the ruins of her dwelling. Fenriis should have left. He knew he should have left. Despite the emperor's shadow ordering him to pick up the Kallson woman, his standing orders *were* from the emperor. He was to do nothing that would jeopardize the upcoming negotiations. Kidnapping a human woman... definitely a problem. Just checking she was okay? Yeah, that fell within his duty of care. Latharian warriors had destroyed her home. It was only right that he check in and make sure she was okay. Make sure none of the assholes were still lingering around to cause problems.

So he moved forward stealthily, still concealed by what remained of a doorway, stopping dead when he heard her whispering. What was she doing? It sounded like she was... praying?

"...I'm not even sure if you're real... I'm desperate. They've got my girls...I'll do anything to get them back. Please... I'll do anything you want... help me..."

He froze in place as the sound of a vicious coughing fit ripped through her. Sneaking a look around the doorframe, he sucked in a hard breath. The tiniest woman he'd ever seen was all but doubled over on the bed, coughing. He couldn't see her face the way she was sitting but... *draanth,* he hadn't realized human women were that tiny. He would be a lumbering brute next to her.

And that cough... he frowned again, concern rolling through him. That cough didn't sound good. It sounded deep and painful. Why hadn't the human healers dealt with that before now? It ripped at his heart to listen to her struggle for breath as the fit ended.

"Please..." she whispered, her voice weak as she sat up. "If anyone is listening, I'll do anything..."

That did it. Fenriis stepped from the door almost before his decision registered. Her eyes were still closed so she didn't pick up on the movement. Stopping a few steps away from her, he deactivated the camouflage on his armor.

It was a bad idea. He *knew* it was a bad idea, but his higher reasoning was not involved here. His instincts had kicked in and all he could see was the tiny little woman sitting in front of him, every primal male urge he had telling him to grab her, throw her over his shoulder and take her back to his ship.

And all that before he'd see her face.

"Anything?" he demanded, the word rougher and coarser than he'd meant it to be.

At the sound of his voice, her head whipped up and she looked at him with utter surprise on her face. A beautiful heart-shaped face with large dark eyes that seemed to see down to his very soul. He froze, hard and ready in an instant, his cock throbbing against the inside of his armor. He instantly discovered that combat armor was *not* the most comfortable thing to be wearing with a raging hard-on.

He'd heard of the human women, of course, what warrior in the empire hadn't? But no one had said how beautiful they were. No wonder the warriors at court were dropping like fucking flies.

"Who ar—" Her gaze dropped to his body armor and the pulse rifle slung across his back. Her eyes widened, her face suddenly pale.

"You're one of them!" Instead of the fright he'd expected, or for her to make a run for it, instead, the tiny human launched herself at him.

"*Youfuckingbastard, yougivemygirlsback!*" she hissed, her arms and legs flailing wildly as she attacked him.

He grunted in surprise as he was forced to counter a surprisingly well-coordinated flurry of blows. Of course, there was no way she could actually *hurt* him, even if he hadn't had his armor on —but someone, somewhere had taught her to fight.

He blocked most of her blows and then clocked

the winces each time she struck his armor and felt a shit because she was hurting herself. Moving with the speed that had earned him a ferocious reputation first on the battlefield and then as a war commander, he ducked the next attack, used her own momentum to swing her around and then came up behind her. It was the work of a second to wrap her up in his arms, yanking her back against his broad, hard chest.

But, instead of admitting she was beaten like a sensible person, she just yelled at him more and arched her back, trying to slam the back of her skull into his nose. He sighed, lifting her off her feet so she couldn't get leverage. His plan worked. Until she started to kick him.

"Getoffmeyoualienbastard!" she shrieked, but he could hear the tears in her voice. It wasn't just frustration... she was heartbroken. Over her children, he realized, processing her earlier words.

"Calm down," he ordered softly as he held her tightly. "I'm not going to hurt you, but you are going to hurt yourself if you carry on."

She spat something unintelligible at him and struggled like a wild thing. Eventually, though, her frantic movement sparked another coughing fit and she couldn't fight him. He loosened his grip, holding her gently and frowning at the vicious spasms that rocked her tiny frame. Finally, she rested back against his chest, her energy spent.

"You said earlier that you'd do anything to get your children back," he murmured quietly, trying hard not to be affected by the softness of her curves against him. He ached to lift a hand and see if the skin of her neck was as soft as it looked, but he resisted the temptation. It might spark a bad reaction, which in turn could set off a coughing fit. He didn't want that. Anyone could see she was running on nothing but nerves and vapor fumes. He'd seen it in warriors on the edge before. She couldn't carry on this way. If she did, she'd make herself very, very ill. And he didn't want that.

"What?" Her voice, now she wasn't yelling at him, was soft and melodic—a pleasant sound higher than the warriors' voices he'd heard all his life. Just listening to her was pleasing to his ears.

"Earlier," he repeated, "when you were talking to your gods. You said you'd do anything your god wanted if he could get your girls back. Was that offer just to your deity?"

She didn't reply at first, but he knew he had all her attention. Her small hands clenched harder where they were clutched around his lower arms for support, her tiny foot wrapped around one of his legs as she teetered on the toes of the other. Off balance, needing him for support. He found he liked the needing him part...

She turned her head, meeting his gaze out of the corner of her eye. He easily read the surprise and the determination on her small features. "I'd do anything to get them back. Anything."

"What if I could get you back to your girls?" he dropped his voice to whisper in her ear. "What would you offer me, given I'm not one of your gods?"

Hope filled her expression. He loosened his grip enough that she could half-turn in his arms and look at him.

"What would you want?" she asked, biting her lip as she studied his face.

He knew he must appear strange to her. Even though his hair was cut short like a lot of human males, that was where the similarity ended. He had the harsh features of his nomad father's clan, black hair and his eyes weren't colored like hers, but dark. So dark they appeared all black, the vertical pupils almost indistinguishable from the irises.

She shivered but didn't scream. He couldn't be that unappealing or frightening to her. Good, because for what he wanted, he really didn't need her to be scared of him.

"I want a mate," he said bluntly. "Accept my claim, become my mate... my wife... and I'll get you back to your daughters."

GET YOUR COPY NOW!

ABOUT THE AUTHOR

Mina Carter is a *New York Times & USA Today* bestselling author of romance in many genres. She lives in the UK with her husband, daughter and a bossy cat.

**WANT THE LATEST NEWS AND CONTESTS?
SIGN UP TO MINA'S NEWSLETTER!**
http://mina-carter.com/newsletter/books/

Connect with Mina online at:
mina-carter.com

- facebook.com/minacarterauthor
- twitter.com/minacarter
- instagram.com/minacarter77
- amazon.com/Mina-Carter
- bookbub.com/authors/mina-carter

Made in the USA
Middletown, DE
26 June 2019